"When am I going

David asked.

"I'm not sure," Kyra answered.

It was her final word on the subject, David realized with an empty feeling in his gut. Were the vows they'd spoken and the rapture they'd shared simply to evanesce like a puff of smoke? Or could they cross the fragile bridge of belief and trust to a life together?

With effort, he remembered his grandfather's counsel. To win Kyra back and keep her for a lifetime, he'd have to be patient. According to his great-grandfather, if her love matched his, she'd remember what had taken place and come back to him. Instead of existing as a memory lost in time, their marriage would unfold in the present moment.

And if she can't? he wondered. *Will I be condemned to walk through life alone, missing the biggest piece of my heart?*

Dear Reader,

This month, Silhouette Romance has six irresistible, emotional and heartwarming love stories for you, starting with our FABULOUS FATHERS title, *Wanted: One Son* by Laurie Paige. Deputy sheriff Nick Dorelli had watched the woman he loved marry another and have that man's child. But now, mother and child need Nick. Next is *The Bride Price* by bestselling author Suzanne Carey. Kyra Martin has fuzzy memories of having just married her Navajo ex-fiancé in a traditional wedding ceremony. And when she discovers she's expecting his child, she knows her dream was not only real…but had mysteriously come true! We also have two not-to-be missed new miniseries starting this month, beginning with *Miss Prim's Untamable Cowboy,* book 1 of THE BRUBAKER BRIDES by Carolyn Zane. A prim image consultant tries to tame a very masculine working-class wrangler into the true Texas millionaire tycoon he really is. Good luck, Miss Prim!

In *Only Bachelors Need Apply* by Charlotte Maclay, a man-shy woman's handsome new neighbor has some secrets that will make her the happiest woman in the world, and in *The Tycoon and the Townie* by Elizabeth Lane, a struggling waitress from the wrong side of the tracks is romanced by a handsome, wealthy bachelor. Finally, our other new miniseries, ROYAL WEDDINGS by Lisa Kaye Laurel. The lovely caretaker of a royal castle finds herself a prince's bride-to-be during a ball…with high hopes for happily ever after in *The Prince's Bride.*

I hope you enjoy all six of Silhouette Romance's terrific novels this month…and every month.

Regards,

Melissa Senate,
Senior Editor

Please address questions and book requests to:
Silhouette Reader Service
U.S.: 3010 Walden Ave., P.O. Box 1325, Buffalo, NY 14269
Canadian: P.O. Box 609, Fort Erie, Ont. L2A 5X3

Suzanne Carey

THE
BRIDE PRICE

Silhouette

R O M A N C E™

Published by Silhouette Books

America's Publisher of Contemporary Romance

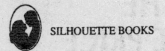

SILHOUETTE BOOKS

ISBN 0-373-19247-9

THE BRIDE PRICE

Printed in U.S.A.

Books by Suzanne Carey

Silhouette Romance

A Most Convenient
  Marriage #633
Run, Isabella #682
Virgin Territory #736
The Baby Contract #777
Home for Thanksgiving #825
Navajo Wedding #855
Baby Swap #880
Dad Galahad #928
Marry Me Again #1001
The Male Animal #1025
The Daddy Project #1072
Father by Marriage #1120
The Bride Price #1247

Silhouette Intimate Moments

Never Say Goodbye #330
Strangers When We Meet #392
True to the Fire #435
Eleanora's Ghost #518
Whose Baby? #715

Silhouette Desire

Kiss and Tell #4
Passion's Portrait #69
Mountain Memory #92
Leave Me Never #126
Counterparts #176
Angel in His Arms #206
Confess to Apollo #268
Love Medicine #310
Any Pirate in a Storm #368

Silhouette Books

Silhouette Summer Sizzlers 1993
"Steam Bath"

SUZANNE CAREY

is a former reporter and magazine editor who prefers to write romance novels because they add to the sum total of love in the world.

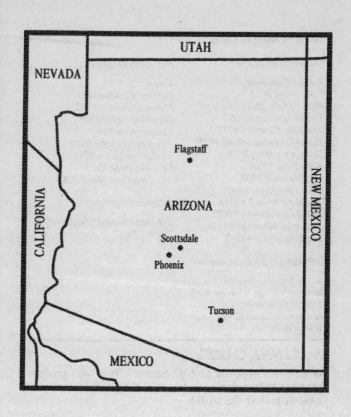

Chapter One

It was 6:22 a.m. on what promised to be a glorious September day. In the bedroom of her Kansas City, Missouri, apartment, Kyra Martin was still deeply asleep as she twisted and turned beneath her down coverlet. Divorced, childless, the twenty-seven-year-old, hardworking assistant federal prosecutor for the Western District of Kansas was immersed in a recurring dream, which had transported her back in time by almost five years to an erotic encounter she'd experienced beneath the graceful torrent of Havasu Falls with David Yazzie, her part-Navajo, would-be lover.

Though in her dream the water was like ice as it plunged about their shoulders, Kyra didn't pay it any heed. Moaning with pleasure and a mounting sense of urgency, she felt her resistance melt as David's mouth crushed hers. The expert way he was teasing her nipples through the fabric of her red bikini top was pushing her past the limits she'd set for herself. If they didn't call a halt, and soon, she'd violate the promise she'd made to herself to remain a virgin until her wedding day.

"David...maybe we'd better stop," she protested when he drew back to gaze at her with lust and longing in his beautiful eyes.

Moving around to her back with the calm audacity that so disarmed and captivated her, his strong, exquisitely shaped fingers tested the clasp on her bra preparatory to unhooking it. "Why should we," he demanded reasonably, "when we both want it so much?"

Mad about him, she found it all but impossible to resist the longing that washed over her in waves as he pressed the front of his swim trunks against her lower body.

A moment later he was unfastening her top and letting it fall into the tumbling waters of the creek that swirled about their ankles. Thanks to the weather, which had turned somewhat chilly, and the fact that it was a weekday, the falls were deserted at that hour except for them. But that ideal state of affairs wouldn't last long. Several of the hikers and campers who haunted the remote but beautiful offshoot of Arizona's Grand Canyon no matter what the season were bound to appear at any moment.

"Please," she managed, begging him to save her from herself, "this is a popular spot. Despite the weather, someone's bound to come along and see us!"

His determination to have her seemingly as fixed as the North Star he'd woven into the retelling of a Native American legend beside their campfire the night before, David nuzzled his kisses lower. "Don't worry," he advised. "Nobody's going to gawk at your beautiful breasts. I'll keep them covered with my hands and mouth...."

Abruptly Kyra's bedside phone rang, shattering the scene her unconscious mind had chosen to present her with in a thousand shining fragments. Jarred and disoriented, with the flush of arousal it had brought to her cheeks slowly fading, she groped for the receiver.

"Hello?" she muttered, rubbing the sleep from her eyes.

"Kyra, it's Dad," her caller announced in his raspy baritone. "Did I wake you, sweetheart?"

Chief prosecutor for Coconino County, Arizona, for more than twenty years, Big Jim Frakes had been widowed for nearly as long. He'd raised Kyra by himself from the time she was eleven. Though he kept close tabs on her even now, he usually called around dinnertime. Something must be up, she thought. About to reassure him that her alarm was set to go off in a few minutes, anyway, she remembered it was a Saturday.

"Sort of," she admitted, propping herself against some pillows. "But I needed to get up, anyway. What can I do for you, Dad?"

The momentary pause was uncharacteristic of him. "Frankly," he said with regret, "I could use a little help."

At sixty-four, and having developed a spot of heart trouble, Big Jim would be retiring soon. Lately he'd begun to make ever more insistent noises about wanting Kyra to return to Flagstaff and work for him—run for election in his stead when his current term was up. The problem was that he had a capable and likeable first assistant, middle-aged Tom Hanrahan, who'd been waiting in the wings for nearly eight years hoping to play that role.

Her father knew how she felt about going head-to-head with Tom. She wouldn't want to do it. She'd told him so half a dozen times, at least. Her other reason for staying away from the town where she'd grown up and the gorgeous sweep of canyon, high desert and pine-clad mountain country she loved so much was one they couldn't talk about. Any mention of David and the fact that he owned a ranch near Flagstaff—one with a striking stone-and-cedar house surrounded by ponderosa pines—would reopen too many wounds.

"Problems at work, Dad?" she asked lightly. "Or is it something of a more personal nature?"

Again she caught that slight hesitation.

"Both, I guess," he admitted at last. "The fact is, I'm faced with trying Paul Naminga for murder. And I—"

Kyra gasped. "Not another tragedy in the Naminga family! I can't believe Paul would ever commit such a crime."

A Hopi paramedic who'd chosen to live and work in Flagstaff rather than remain in the Second Mesa village of Mishongnovi on the reservation where he'd been raised, Paul Naminga was known and liked in both the Anglo and Native American communities. Still, the family had a history of trouble. Five years earlier, Paul's mildly retarded, alcoholic older brother, Leonard, had been on trial on charges of manslaughter, grand theft auto and driving under the influence. It had been during this trial that Kyra, then a second-year law student, and David Yazzie, who'd been employed as the first-ever Native American assistant on Big Jim's staff, had gotten to know each other.

Because the alleged crimes had taken place off the reservation, a short distance from the Lariat Bar on Route 89 north of town, the case had been prosecuted in state rather than federal court. Despite Leonard's frantic, somewhat garbled denials of any wrongdoing, all the available evidence had pointed to him. He'd been found drunk and confused behind the wheel of Dale Cargill's pickup truck, which had been reported missing by its owner a short time earlier. At some point prior to the arrival of the sheriff's deputies on the scene, the truck had plowed into a shabby sedan, killing both occupants, a local man and woman in their late sixties.

Off for the summer, Kyra had volunteered to help with the case, which, while tragic, had seemed basically open-and-shut. Slowly, however, both she and David had begun to wonder whether Leonard Naminga might be innocent. Sublimating their loyalty to Big Jim, they'd done their best to check out their hunch.

The effort had come to nothing. Leonard had been convicted, anyway, and sent off to state prison. A few days later David had quit Big Jim's staff and walked out of Kyra's life without a word or a backward glance, leaving her stunned and heartsick. The resulting downward spiral of her emotions had threatened to sink her third-year grade point average.

At least, it had until her father had explained the part he'd played in David's disappearance. Shamefacedly he'd confessed to bribing the man Kyra loved with ten thousand dollars to dump her—for her own good. He'd justified the costly, underhanded move by arguing that he'd wanted her to finish law school and establish a legal career for herself instead of dropping out to get married and have David Yazzie's babies.

She'd refused to believe it in the beginning. Told him he was lying, that David would never stoop so low. It was only when he'd shown her the entry in his checkbook, explaining that the canceled check hadn't been returned to him yet, that she'd begun to think it possible. Sobbing that she wouldn't have dropped out if David had asked her to marry him, Kyra had refused to speak to her father for several months.

Only later had she become suspicious that, despite Big Jim's apparent liking for David, and his frequently stated admiration for the handsome young assistant prosecutor's savvy and toughness, his real reason for attempting to break them up had stemmed from the fact that David was part Native American. She'd been furious with both men—David for selling her out and her father for his unstated prejudice.

She'd finally forgiven the latter after numerous abject apologies on his part. No apologies or communication of any kind had been forthcoming from David. Though she'd married fellow law graduate Brad Martin on the rebound and divorced him three and a half years later because they'd had nothing in common, not even their principles, the pain and deep sense of loneliness David had caused by accepting her father's bribe remained the major hurt in her heart.

It still rankled with her that he'd almost certainly used the money to set up a shoestring legal practice, parlaying it into a highly successful career. In the five years since they'd seen each other, he'd made a name for himself representing clients of modest means, many of them Native American, against the government and wealthy corporations. In the process, he'd won some spectacular judgments. Lately he'd begun to be quoted as a legal expert on television.

He stepped over me on his way to fame and fortune, Kyra thought. Yet, who can blame him? Asked to make a choice, he embraced what mattered to him most. She only wished his fleeting, unconsummated romance with the county attorney's daughter had occupied a more important place in his heart.

Now Paul Naminga's life and liberty were at stake. "Who's Paul supposed to have killed?" she asked, pushing down the heartsick feeling that always troubled her when thoughts of David surfaced.

"Ben Monongye," Big Jim was saying. "You remember him…the thickset Hopi with the scarred right cheek who put together a successful construction business with the help of federal set-asides for minorities."

Kyra did. Though she'd admired Ben's hard work and tough-mindedness, she'd always thought him a little brash and self-seeking. From what she'd heard via the grapevine, he'd considered himself something of a Casanova with the ladies.

"He and Paul were both scheduled to perform in the Hopi segment of a multitribe dance festival that was held on the Museum of Northern Arizona grounds last weekend," her father continued. "Apparently Ben had been hitting on Paul's wife, Julie. He and Paul traded blows about it shortly before they were due to put on their costumes. We've got umpteen witnesses."

Frowning, Kyra tried to picture the scene.

"A couple of bystanders broke it up," Big Jim said. "Paul ordered Ben to stay away from Julie and stalked off toward his trailer. Ben went into another trailer to dress. He never showed up onstage. Though he made it, Paul was late. During the dancing, a couple of kids fishing around in the trailers for loose change discovered Ben's body."

"The fact that Paul was late for the performance doesn't prove he was the killer," Kyra objected. "There could have been any number of reasons...."

She could almost see her father shaking his head.

"I know you like Paul," he said, sighing. "I do, too. But Red Miner was right to make the arrest. There's just too much evidence against him."

Red Miner was the Coconino County sheriff.

"Give me a 'for instance,'" Kyra requested.

"Okay, sure. Take the minute spatters of blood the crime-scene techs found on Paul's *Koyemsi* costume. Preliminary analysis suggests it matches Ben's, and I'm betting the DNA report will confirm it. Plus a young girl came forward to say she saw someone costumed like Paul go into Ben's trailer after everyone headed for the bleachers."

He paused. "Of course, her testimony doesn't make it an open-and-shut case. As you probably remember, unlike the sacred clown dancers, the *Koyemsi* are masked. We don't have an eyewitness, as such.''

The thought that maybe Paul didn't do it settled a little deeper into Kyra's consciousness. It was like a replay of what had happened to his brother, she thought. Most of the evidence was circumstantial.

"Paul claims he's innocent," Big Jim said. "That he was late for the performance because some Navajo kid ran up to him as he was about to get dressed and begged him to come revive one of his friends, who'd been sniffing glue. Unfortunately we couldn't locate any of the boys to corroborate his story."

In all likelihood, her father was right. The blood on the costume would match Ben's. And the evidence would pile up. Lacking another suspect, a jury would convict Paul. It didn't look good for him.

Meanwhile, Big Jim hadn't explained what kind of help he wanted. Her heart sank a moment later when he let it be known that David Yazzie had taken charge of Paul's defense.

Her dream taking on the aura of a premonition, Kyra conjured a mental picture of David's broad shoulders and slim hips. How she'd loved the brilliant flash of smile that could illuminate his tanned, chiseled features like sunlight breaking through storm clouds over a distant mesa. And his hands. Oh, his hands…

"This will likely be my last big case," her father was saying. "I don't want to lose it, especially not to him. With your help—"

The prospect of running into David on the street had been enough to keep Kyra's visits to her hometown to a minimum. Now she was supposed to return voluntarily, battle it out with him in the courtroom, face-to-face?

"What about Tom Hanrahan?" she said. "Surely he can give you all the help you need."

"Sorry. But he can't, honey. Tom's hospitalized in Missoula, Montana…in traction with a broken leg. He got injured on a hunting trip. He'll be out of the picture for quite a while."

He hadn't said so, yet Kyra guessed her father thought David would be gunning for him. Though David might have taken her father's money and run with it five years earlier, he wouldn't have thanked him for making the offer. Despite his own mercenary behavior he'd have been deeply insulted to realize Big Jim didn't consider his mixed Navajo, Hispanic and Anglo blood good enough for his daughter—whether or not he'd ever had serious designs on her.

"I remember you mentioning recently that you've accrued a mountain of compensatory time," her father said. "If it wouldn't be too much of a hardship, I wish you could take some of it off. Come down to Flag and help me prosecute."

Kyra realized he was probably hoping her presence on the prosecution team would rattle David, create sufficient tension to give the prosecution an edge. However, she was well aware of his respect for her ability. Thanks to her experience in the Office of the U.S. Attorney, she was Tom Hanrahan's equal at the very least.

Dad's getting older, she thought. And tired. He wants to go out with his head up. Maybe because of David's reputation as an attorney who doesn't take many cases he can't win, his faith in his ability to do that has become a little shaky.

Much as she wanted to help, she wasn't ready to see David again. Her hurt over his betrayal, and her heart's stubborn inability to get over him, still ran deep. Still, she'd just put an important case to bed. And she *had* been working a lot of seventy-hour weeks. She didn't want her father to realize David was still a burr under her saddle. She could, she supposed, drive down, go over his brief for him, suggest some arguments.

"You know I want to help," she hedged. "But I'll have to talk to my boss before making any promises. We've got a lot of important work coming up. If he can spare me, maybe we can work something out."

Clearly pleased that she hadn't turned him down flat, Big Jim promised to call her Monday night. "I'll be mighty appreciative of whatever you can do to help," he said. "No doubt it's a proud father speaking. But you took to prosecuting like a duck to water. With Tom laid up in Missoula, I couldn't do better than to have you on my side."

Putting down the receiver after exchanging a few more words with him, Kyra headed for the shower. Inevitably, as she shampooed her sun-streaked blond hair and scrubbed her body with foaming jojoba-scented gel, the spray brought back her dream of Havasu Falls and all the volatile, half-buried emotions it had evoked. In a couple of weeks, if Big Jim had his way, she'd be seeing David again— gazing into stunning eyes capable of undressing her soul and extracting its every secret.

Unwillingly, because she didn't want to fall under his spell again, she imagined herself running her fingers through his thick, sweet-smelling hair, which was as sensuous to the touch as coarse, black silk. How she'd loved being crushed by his powerful arms. Kissed everywhere she'd allowed his libidinous mouth to wander.

Just to watch him address a jury, smolderingly handsome in a business suit and tie, or sauntering toward her in faded jeans with the bred-in-the-bone grace of his Native American ancestors and a knowing grin on his face had caused her to thank God every morning that she was young, female and relatively good-looking in the world he inhabited.

She thought of his powerful sexual allure and her apprehension over his formidable reputation as a defense attorney who seemed to possess an extraordinary talent for unraveling the facts of a case. Though she tried to shake them off, these memories clung to Kyra as she tugged on jeans, a sweatshirt and a windbreaker to jog in a park near her home and go about her Saturday errands.

Though his morals hadn't extended to refusing her father's bribe, David apparently was unswerving in his demand that the clients he accepted be guiltless and/or deserving of redress, according to several newspaper and journal articles she'd read about him. If that's true, he must believe in Paul Naminga's innocence, since he agreed to defend him, she acknowledged as she unloaded a week's worth of groceries at the checkout counter of her favorite supermarket. Her father's job as prosecutor was going to be tough despite the evidence Red Miner had collected.

When Kyra broached the matter of a sabbatical with her boss, U.S. Attorney Jonathan Hargrave, on Monday, he insisted she take as much time as she needed to help her father. "You've been driving yourself way too hard," he lectured her. "I don't want you to burn out. Or fall prey to some stress-related ailment. Take a breather…six weeks at least, more if you need it…and do what you can for your dad. You might even try smelling a few roses."

Her father was elated when she gave him the news. "You'll never know how much I appreciate this, honey," he said.

They worked it out that she'd drive down to Flagstaff two weeks hence, in time for the exchange of discovery between the defense and the prosecution.

"You don't need to sit in on the discovery session unless you want to," her father said, in deference to what he probably realized were her strong misgivings. "Of course, I'm hoping you'll choose to be present. You're damn good at sniffing out the weaknesses in a defense case, you know. You might pick up on something I miss."

He wants me there to throw David off base, she thought again, her earlier speculation strengthening. He doesn't realize that, despite my anger over the shabby way David treated me, a part of me still yearns for him. Or else his fear of going out a loser is pretty strong. Whatever the reason for his comments, Kyra reflected, it was narrowly possible that her going wouldn't be a mistake. While it was too much to expect that she'd feel nothing when she and the part-Navajo defense attorney she'd once loved came face-to-face, she might use the moment as a springboard for getting over him.

Three days later, thirty-six-year-old David Yazzie was currying his favorite saddle horse, Born for Water, outside the barn on his *Yebetchai* Ranch. A little tired, having just come off a case himself—one that he'd resolved in his client's favor—he was glad to be home again. Living out of the motor home that became both office and sleeping quarters when he was on the road pleading cases in Wyoming, North Dakota or New Mexico was okay, he guessed. But it didn't give him the sense of peace and rootedness he felt on his three-hundred-plus acreage studded with ponderosa pine and juniper. With all his heart he loved the ranch and the house he'd built of stone and cedar to his own specifications in the shadow of the sacred mountains.

So why did he feel so restless this morning? he wondered.

Most of what he consciously wanted was within his reach. From impoverished beginnings on the reservation, as the son of a widowed, mostly Navajo mother and a father of mixed Navajo, Anglo and Hispanic background, who'd been killed in a railroad accident before his birth, he'd come a long way. Thanks to the U.S. Army, which he'd joined in order to be eligible for the G.I. Bill, he'd earned a bachelor's degree, then begged and borrowed his way into law school.

After serving as one of Jim Frakes's assistants in Flag to establish some credentials for himself, he'd gone on to create a way of life that included a good income—by virtue of his successful lawsuits against negligent corporations—and the satisfaction of helping deserving underdogs win vindication or redress.

In many ways he'd achieved the best of what the Anglo world had to offer. Meanwhile, his Native American ancestors had bequeathed him a rich spiritual heritage. From his great-grandfather, who'd died of advanced old age several years earlier, he'd learned ancient medicine man secrets known only to a few, which allowed him to step beyond the distortions of the present and get at the hidden truth in situations.

Yet something fundamental was missing from his day-to-day existence. He felt it most whenever he finished a case and returned to Flag, with enough leisure to step back from the quotidian flow of work and think about his situation.

This time, because of the trouble that had befallen Paul Naminga, there wouldn't be much time for reflection. Yet the prospect of defending the Hopi paramedic in what would probably be Jim Frakes's last major case hadn't assuaged his yearning.

A chance discovery had only made it worse. While going through some notes David had saved from the Leonard Naminga trial on his first night home, he'd run across a group snapshot taken in the county attorney's office on the occasion of Tom Hanrahan's fortieth birthday. In the picture, a smiling, slightly younger version of himself stood with his arm around slim, blond Kyra Frakes—Martin now, he reminded himself. Bronze in contrast to the freckled paleness of her skin, his fingers curled about her upper arm, which was bared by her sleeveless blouse.

He'd almost been able to smell the perfume she wore, feel the heat and vitality that radiated from her body as he stared at the photograph. *I shouldn't have let Jim talk me into walking out on her that way*, he thought now, by the corral, for perhaps the thousandth time. *I could have helped her finish law school—made whatever sacrifices it took. As husband and wife, we'd have lit up the sky with a fire that would be still burning.*

If she cared at all after so much time had passed, that caring took the form of aversion, he guessed. He supposed he could count himself lucky that she wouldn't be around during the trial to make the besotted thirty-year-old inside him, whose memories were alive and well, eat his heart out. Being civil to the former boss who'd wanted him out of her life for what in retrospect he considered offensive reasons would be difficult enough.

Finishing with the horse, David patted the glossy animal's neck and led him to his stall. He was just closing the stall gate when the cellular phone in his hip pocket chirped.

His caller turned out to be Jim Frakes's secretary since time immemorial, Jody Ann Daniels. "Hey, gorgeous. How ya doin'?" the fortyish mother of three greeted him. "The boss asked me to call and set up the discovery exchange in *State v. Naminga* for a week from Monday. That fit with your schedule?"

He hadn't been able to do his usual thorough investigation yet. "So long as he's willing to revisit if and when new information comes to light," he conceded.

Jody Ann laughed outright. "Knowing you'd ask, he so

stipulated. By the way...your old friend Kyra's taking a leave of absence from her high-powered Kansas City job to help her pop, what with Tom Hanrahan bedridden in Missoula. Guess she's a little freer to flit around the country, now that she's divorced. It's gonna be like old home week around here!''

Kyra was divorced. She was coming back to Flagstaff.

Folding the phone and slipping it back in his pocket after saying goodbye to Jody, David walked back to the corral and leaned over the fence. He rested the astonishing blue gaze he'd inherited from Anglo ancestors on his father's side and W. W. Trask, the legendary Irish-American–Native American scout who'd been his mother's great-great-great-grandfather, against the mountains' enduring beauty.

Did he still have a chance with her? His thoughts in turmoil, he found himself staring into the void his estrangement from Kyra had created. Though he'd tried to phone her a year after they'd parted, around the time she'd graduated, he·hadn't been able to reach her. Soon afterward he'd heard she had been married. After that the notion of contacting her had seemed pointless.

They hadn't talked or even glimpsed each other in passing since the day her father had pressured him into leaving her for her own good, and he'd been fool enough to swallow the bait.

Now fate had taken a hand.

Seeing her again will either cure me or reinfect me with the same old yearning, he thought. As he pondered what to do about it, a remark his mother's grandfather had once made drifted through his head. *You can't change the past, even if you acquire the wisdom to visit it,* Henry Many Horses had observed in his quiet way. *But you can learn a great deal from the lessons it has to teach.*

Chapter Two

Thanks to a last-minute flurry of activity in Kansas City, where she was pressed into taking depositions for another assistant who had the flu, Kyra wasn't able to leave until noon on Saturday. I probably won't make it to Flag in time for the discovery exchange, she thought as she headed southwest on Interstate 35 toward Wichita in her cherry red Jeep Cherokee. And I'll miss my first opportunity to come face-to-face with David. It's almost as if I *planned* it that way.

Kyra didn't bargain on the fact that her compulsion to see him again would build as the miles racked up, causing her to press her foot a little harder on the gas pedal. By the time she reached Gallup, New Mexico, late Sunday afternoon, her yearning to see him and the strong apprehension that gripped her at the prospect were at each other's throats. Within striking distance, she decided to stop early.

More alone in a roadside café and her motel room than she customarily felt in her Kansas City apartment, she tossed and turned that night, getting very little sleep. Finally, around 5 a.m., she gave it up, showered and dressed and headed for the checkout desk.

She arrived in Flagstaff shortly after 9 a.m., the appointed hour for the informal exchange of discovery in *State of Arizona v. Naminga* to start. Parking the Cherokee in a recently vacated spot and getting out to smooth her beige wool gabardine suit and neat French-braided chignon, she couldn't quell her nervousness.

What if I'm still in love with him after all this time? she tormented herself. I don't think I could bear it. I have a right to get over him—to learn to be happy with someone else.

With its prominent clock tower, the red sandstone courthouse where her father's office was situated had long been a Flagstaff landmark. The dark-paneled lobby, with its murky portraits in oil and broad, imposing staircase leading to the second floor, was just as she remembered it. Only the anteroom to his private lair had changed. If possible, it appeared to be even more choked with files and papers.

"Long time no see," Jody Ann Daniels greeted her, interrupting her typing to give Kyra her usual insouciant grin. "I hate to say it, but you look better every time I see you. The meeting got started a few minutes ago. Your dad said to tell you that if you made it in time, you were to go right in."

Her heart in her throat, Kyra entered her father's office, which hadn't changed much since her childhood. Law books and Zane Gray novels still filled the shelves. Paintings of cowboys and hunting trophies crowded the walls, reflecting the bluff, plainspoken county attorney's interests. A pair of skis he hadn't used for a decade reposed in one corner, gathering dust.

Keenly conscious of David's presence and the fact that he'd risen to his feet, Kyra postponed acknowledging him as she returned her father's affectionate squeeze and greeted the court reporter he'd summoned, whom she'd known since high school.

At last, swallowing, she turned to face the man she'd snubbed, who owned the lion's share of her attention.

So surprising against the palette of his coppery skin and coal black hair, David's light, beautiful eyes seemed to burn with a fire that had something hidden at its heart. All the lectures she'd given herself notwithstanding, she wanted to drown in them, offer to be his hostage.

"Kyra," he said simply in his soft, deep voice, holding out his hand to her.

If she was to maintain any semblance of control over the situation, she had to take it. Grasped lightly, it was firm, callused and warm enough to send little shivers of awareness racing up her arms. Every kiss they'd exchanged, every intimacy she'd permitted him in her formerly besotted state, seemed to hover between them in memory, suggesting renewed, even more passionate congress.

"Hello...good to see you again," she murmured, realizing too late how idiotic and awkward the words must sound. They were hardly strangers. Or even mere acquaintances.

Holding her captive a moment longer than necessary, David responded that it was good to see her, too. She'd been a girl when he'd left. Now she was a woman. Another man had initiated her. With a fierceness he didn't let show, he longed to step back in time and undo that hurt, claim the priceless opportunity he'd missed for himself.

He'd never been able to manage the first half of that equation where she was concerned. His feelings always got in the way. As for changing things, he'd long since learned that only the future held possibilities.

For her part, Kyra was overwhelmed by his quiet power

and almost mystical resonance. In the years they'd been apart, he seemed to have acquired a depth and maturity that were stunning for a man in his mid-thirties. How can someone whose loyalties were so shifting, so available for purchase, project such an aura of decency and wisdom? she asked herself.

There didn't seem to be any answer. Meanwhile, his physical magnetism was overpowering her. Though he was dressed for his lawyer's role in a charcoal gray suit, white shirt and tie, she couldn't help but imagine him in faded, slightly shrunken blue jeans. Compared to him, the husband she'd divorced and the men she'd dated since were ciphers—pallid imitations of the standard he'd set.

Somehow she had to resist if he tried to jump-start their romance. Remembering the money he took ought to do it, she thought bitterly. In her experience, the principles he claimed to espouse were so much poppycock.

Conscious her father was watching her for signs that she was still susceptible, she shuttered her feelings and pulled a worn wooden chair up to one corner of his desk. "Please...don't let me interrupt," she murmured. "I assume no one will mind if I take a few notes."

In Arizona an "open file" rule prevailed, in which both sides in a criminal case could consult a list maintained by the county clerk in which the opposing attorneys catalogued the evidence they planned to present and their proposed witnesses. However, Kyra's father had always held discovery meetings. He claimed to like the give-and-take, the small-town camaraderie, not to mention the chance to pick up some tidbit of information or other he couldn't have accessed by any other means.

Taking up where he'd left off, Big Jim continued to run down his list of witnesses. It turned out to be a lengthy one, given the number of people who'd seen Paul Naminga and Ben Monongye trade blows outside the latter's trailer. Many of the names, both Anglo and Native American, were familiar to her. However, she didn't know the young girl who'd seen a man in Paul's costume go into Ben's trailer.

Moving on to the preliminary tests investigators had conducted on the bloodstains, he offered David a copy of the lab report. "Something else has, uh, come up," her father added in a tone that alerted Kyra he regarded it as a chink in his armor. "The crime scene unit found several hairs in the trailer where Ben Monongye was stabbed that don't match his or Paul's. Their natural color seems to have been black-gray...."

David frowned with interest. "You say *natural?*"

"Turns out they were coated with black hair dye. Of course, they could have been shed in the trailer at some point before the murder took place...maybe even weeks earlier. On the day of the performance, lots of people were in and out of those trailers. Besides, they were rentals. No telling where they'd been before Suzy Horvath rented them."

Suzy Horvath, a forty-something divorcee who owned and edited a local tabloid, had organized the dance festival. Out of the corner of her eye, Kyra caught David's quick flash of smile.

"Thanks," he said, the grooves beside his mouth deepening. "That's a little bit of evidence we can work with."

Big Jim shrugged, hiding any concern he might feel. "I don't think it's going to amount to much."

They were almost finished when Judge Beamish, who would preside over Paul's case, sauntered in from his chambers down the hall to perch on a windowsill. Though he didn't interrupt, he gave Kyra a smile and nod of recognition. A moment or two later, he was followed by a bailiff, who'd brought the handcuffed defendant over from his cell in the nearby jail.

So there's to be a bail hearing, too, Kyra realized, exchanging a silent hello with the clean-cut, boyish-looking paramedic. Seeing Paul again made it all the more difficult to believe he was guilty of murder, despite his public confrontation with the victim.

Watching the wheels turn in her head, David picked up on her sympathies as surely as if she'd laid them out for him on her father's desk. She's just the same, he marveled. Decent. Fair-minded. A champion of the underdog if it was merited. Despite her experience as a prosecutor, he could tell she was still an ethical defense attorney at heart.

If they'd married, as Kyra had wanted them to when they were working together on the Leonard Naminga case, they'd probably have slept *and* worked together. The happiness in his life would have been seamless. By now, they might even have become parents, he thought. Aware the heat of his regard was making her uncomfortable, David forced himself to pay attention.

As he marshaled his arguments for Paul's release and Big Jim countered them, the buildup of tension in Kyra's neck and shoulders from attempting to sit gracefully erect and pretend David was part of the furniture became excruciating.

At last it was Judge Beamish's turn to speak. Citing the capital nature of the crime, he denied David's request.

Excusing himself with a long, slow look at Kyra, David accompanied his client and the bailiff back to the jail so that he and Paul could hold a private conference.

For Kyra, it was as if all the light and energy in the room had departed with him. He didn't bother to say goodbye, she thought. But then, why should he? There's no precedent. A small, still voice inside her whispered, *The twenty-*

two-year-old girl you once were was hoping he regretted his mistake, that he would try to win you back.

It was going to be a long six weeks. Slumping a little in her chair, she tried to center herself.

An informal bull session followed between her dad and the judge, a burly, fifty-something widower. Only half paying attention, Kyra was stunned to hear Hank Beamish remark that he and David were dating the same woman—Suzy Horvath, the newspaper editor who'd organized the dance festival.

"We're not really rivals, of course," he confided with a wink at her. "So there's no ground for prejudice. I don't need to recuse myself."

If Big Jim found the conversation a little awkward, in view of Kyra's presence, he didn't let it show. "How's that, Hank?" he asked negligently.

The judge laughed outright as he stood and smoothed down his robe. "Hell, Suzy would tumble for him in a minute, if she thought he was serious. Of course, she's a couple of years older than him. But that doesn't mean much nowadays."

Why should I feel as if a knife has been plunged into the softest part of my stomach? Kyra asked herself. *It's just gossip, after all. I should have expected something of the sort. David's had a lot of women since I refused to surrender my virginity without marriage. And he'll have a lot more. It's no skin off my nose.*

Her heart stubbornly aching despite the brave words she'd summoned to comfort herself, Kyra bade Judge Beamish goodbye and spent a few additional minutes hugging and talking to her dad. However, when an important phone call came through for him, she decided she'd had enough of hanging around the courthouse for one morning. Her parking meter had probably expired, anyway. Scribbling him a note that she planned to drive out to the house and take a dip in the pool, after stopping to see Red Miner's wife, Flossie, who'd all but adopted her when her mother died, she headed for the stairs.

In the interim, David had finished with his client and headed back in search of her. He came striding into the shadowed, momentarily deserted lobby just as she reached the bottom of the stairs. There was nobody around to form opinions or take notes.

"Forget something?" she asked as casually as she could, taking a tentative step toward the door.

His blue eyes glittered against the tan of his face. "As a matter of fact, I did. And I came back for it."

She realized abruptly that he was blocking her exit. "Dad's still upstairs if you need to talk to him," she whispered.

"It isn't your Dad I came back to see. And I suspect you know it, Changing Woman."

It was one of the love names he'd used for her. Beneath her staid, lawyerly suit, Kyra was tingling all over.

"David, I don't think..." she began.

He wasn't thinking, either. He was leading with his heart. Cutting off her flow of words before she could say something to discourage what he wanted, he tugged her to him and covered her mouth with his, boldly inserting his tongue.

To be in his arms again, thigh to thigh and mouth to mouth, was like regaining a missing part of herself. Passion rose in a flood, racing through the parched arroyos of her loneliness like the male rain of a summer deluge anointing the high desert. The taste of him, both salty and sweet, his clean remembered scent of piñon and musk invading her nostrils, nearly blew her away.

Yes, oh yes, she thought helplessly. This is what I've

needed. What I've longed for with every breath, despite his treachery.

Pliant as an aspen shedding its leaves on an October mountainside, she didn't pull away. He was the first to break contact. Holding her back from him, though he continued to grip her upper arms, he gazed down at her with a gamut of emotions on his face.

"Kyra, Kyra," he said softly. "You'll never know...."

Abruptly, there were footsteps on the stairs behind them. One of the typists from the county clerk's office gave them a sidelong glance as she brushed past them and hurried down the hall, her high heels clicking on the tiles.

The woman was known to be something of a gossip. Wrenching free, Kyra regarded David with fire in her eyes. Her delicate, ringless hands had settled belligerently on her hips.

"How dare you do...what you just did, after the way you walked out on me five years ago?" she demanded, unconsciously offering him a full confession of how badly he'd wounded her. "Surely you realize you're the last man in the world I'd have anything to do with!"

It wasn't the time or the place to engage her in a shouting match. He wanted to make love to her, not fight over past mistakes. If she wanted an apology, he'd be glad to give it. He shouldn't have left as he did. He'd realized that a hundred miles down the road.

He just couldn't let the falsehood stand. "You know you wanted me to kiss you...that we both wanted it," he asserted in his soft, deep voice.

It was true, God help her. One glimpse of him, one touch, and she was burning up with need for him.

She'd never confess the truth—not if she lived to be a hundred. Turning on her heel without a word, she walked out the courthouse door. He didn't follow. She didn't have to turn around to know that he was staring after her.

Pulling herself together, she strode toward her Cherokee with the energy of ten. She supposed it was too much to hope that Cheryl Garcia, the typist who'd caught them kissing, wouldn't spread the story around. Though it was the county seat, Flagstaff was still a small town. Most people knew each other. It wouldn't be long before everyone thought they were having an affair.

Furious with David for putting her in that position and even angrier at herself, Kyra unlocked the door on the driver's side. She almost didn't see the sweet-faced young woman who'd just emerged from the county jail, a few paces down the street.

"Kyra...Kyra Frakes...is that you?" the woman called, motioning her to wait.

Thoughts of David and her tangled feelings for him faded. The woman was Paul Naminga's wife, Julie. They'd met five years earlier, during the Leonard Naminga case. It was safe to say that, at the moment, she had more crushing burdens than Kyra did.

"Julie...I was so sorry to hear about what happened," she said earnestly when they were face-to-face. "I've always liked Paul so much...."

Though Julie Naminga's tone was cool, it didn't ring with censure or condemnation. "I understand you're here to help your father prosecute him," she said.

Kyra wasn't sure how to respond. For some reason she felt incredibly guilty. Yet she hadn't done anything. "Dad phoned and asked for my help, since Tom Hanrahan is out of commission," she answered a bit defensively. "Since I happen to love him, I said yes."

A licensed practical nurse at the local hospital, Julie didn't attempt to soothe her with polite clichés. Or launch into a diatribe. Instead, she seemed simply to absorb Kyra's explanation and accept it for what it was—the reason she'd chosen to give for her actions. She's reacting as David might have, in her place, Kyra realized.

"I'd like to say something for the record," Julie told her after a moment. "My husband's innocent, just as Leonard was. When you and David were helping your father prosecute *him*, you sensed he wasn't responsible for that elderly couple's death. And you did what you could to find out the truth instead of pushing for a conviction."

Kyra bit her lip. "You're right. We did," she admitted. "We weren't very successful, I'm afraid."

Again, Julie didn't attempt to reassure her with platitudes. The fact that they'd failed was the simple truth. There could be no denying or glossing over it.

"I don't expect you to switch sides...join in the defense," she said. "Just that you'll give my husband the same chance you gave Leonard, by keeping your eyes and ears open for holes in your father's case. Or conflicting evidence."

Kyra felt keenly that she was being put on the spot. "I can't act as an informer for David Yazzie," she said reprovingly.

"I'm not asking for that. Just that you keep an open mind."

A loose strand of Kyra's hair blew in her face and she brushed it back. "I like to think I'm capable of that."

"Then you'll do it?"

Kyra nodded. "Yes."

They stood there, looking at each other for a moment.

"Any idea who might have wanted to kill Ben Monongye, if not Paul?" Kyra asked.

Julie Naminga laughed bitterly. "Lots of people," she

said, tossing off some names that ran the gamut from Anglo to Native American.

Though she'd been gone quite a while, Kyra knew most of them. One name that stood out was that of Dale Cargill, the forty-three-year-old, unmarried son of Roy and Betty Cargill, semiretired ranchers who were lifelong friends of her dad's. Awkward, a loner given to gambling, tasteless jokes and drinking too much, Dale ran his father's former construction business, which she'd heard hadn't been doing too well of late.

In that role, he'd been a business rival of the victim's. Coincidentally, he was also the owner of the pickup truck that Paul's brother, Leonard, had allegedly stolen shortly before crashing it into the elderly couple's Pontiac five years earlier, and killing them.

The oddly synchronous details didn't appear to have any significance. Though she'd always considered Dale somewhat offbeat, and found his penchant for mooning over her distasteful, Kyra doubted he'd hurt a flea. With relief—because she liked his parents—she dismissed him as a suspect.

Bidding Julie goodbye, she got into the Cherokee and drove east, toward the country club and the area of better homes that surrounded it. Before heading for the one where she'd grown up, with its four big bedrooms, heated swimming pool and choice view of the mountains, she'd stop to see Flossie Miner, as planned. Favorite aunt, substitute mom and lifelong family friend rolled into one, plump, bespectacled Flossie was always good for what ailed her.

Apparently Big Jim had phoned to let her know Kyra was coming.

"Don't you look nice, all duded up in your lawyer's suit with your hair in that pretty braid!" Flossie exclaimed, popping out of her front door and holding out her arms, before Kyra could switch off the Cherokee's engine.

"I imagine you've heard that you and your dad are scheduled to be our guests for dinner at the country club tonight," Flossie said as she led Kyra to the patio for coffee and Danish. "What you may not realize is that, as of this coming Thursday, your dad will have worked in the Office of the County Attorney for forty years. That's right! He started as a twenty-four-year-old fresh out of law school. In honor of the occasion, some of us have decided to throw him a little party tonight."

Delighted for her father's sake, Kyra fretted that she didn't have a present for him.

"Not to worry," Flossie reassured. "To avoid a wedding shower atmosphere, which would embarrass him, we've gotten together on a group gift...that expensive new set of golf clubs he's been wanting. No stuffy gold watches for Big Jim!"

Though Kyra had spent very little time in Flagstaff since David had walked out on her, she and Flossie had stayed in close contact. She knew the older woman could keep a confidence. As a result, she decided to share some, though not all, of her feelings about seeing David again.

Sympathetic as always, Flossie patted her hand. "As I recall, the two of you made a handsome couple back in the days when you both worked on your daddy's staff," she said. "I guess you've heard he dates Suzy Horvath now when he's in town. As a matter of fact, the grapevine has it that she's bringing him tonight. Still, it wouldn't surprise me that, if you crooked your little finger..."

Kyra blushed, remembering David's kiss in the courthouse lobby. "I may have been madly in love with him five years ago," she admitted. "But that was then. This is now. As far as I'm concerned, Suzy can have him. I'll never forgive or forget the way he walked out on me. It can't be put right.''

Heading home to her father's house a few blocks away, she tried to take a nap. But she couldn't get David out of her thoughts. With all her heart, she longed to confront him. Demand to know why he'd accepted a bribe to leave her. I'd like to hear him try to square *that* with his precious ethics, she thought.

She realized she'd never ask. Letting him know she still cared to that extent would be just too humiliating. It was a mercy when her dad came home and they had a little time to chat before she had to go upstairs and dress.

Returning to her former room, which was still decorated with the cream-colored bed linens and gentian-blue-flowered wallpaper she'd chosen as a teenager, Kyra realized she hadn't brought much in the way of party clothes. When she laid them out on the bed, the few dress-up outfits she'd packed seemed to lack interest.

I have no intention of working my wiles on David—just putting Suzy Horvath in her place and making him eat his heart out, she told herself forcefully as she rummaged in the back of her walk-in closet. A moment later she'd found what she was looking for, a short-sleeved, two-piece cock-tail dress in sapphire blue crepe de chine that followed her every curve and accentuated her Scandinavian-blond hair. She'd worn it once for David when he was romancing her. And it had knocked his socks off.

When she tried it on, it still fit perfectly. The only difference was that, with a few years' maturity under her belt, she filled the plunging sweetheart neckline with a little more cleavage. With a bitter nod of satisfaction, she hung the dress in readiness on the back of the closet door and slipped into the shower to perfume and pamper herself.

* * *

At the party, despite all the compliments and friendly greetings that came her way, Kyra found it difficult to control her jealousy when David entered the room with Suzy on his arm. Though the redheaded newspaperwoman was in her early forties, at least, she was still quite attractive, in Kyra's opinion. It was all she could do to make small talk with her dinner companions—her dad, the Miners, Dale Cargill and his parents—and keep from glancing in their direction.

Following the meal, Red Miner sprung the surprise aspect of the get-together when he arose and offered a toast. A little red in the face from all the spontaneous applause and humorous anecdotes that followed, Big Jim couldn't keep from wiping away a tear when Red presented him with his much-coveted golf clubs.

"You really shouldn't have," he said, gazing around the room at all his friends, and then laughing, added, "but I'm mighty glad you did. I've been eyeing these darn things... and trying to justify buying them...for months!"

Following her father's speech, which included a plug for get-well cards to be sent to his temporarily disabled assistant, Tom Hanrahan, along with an announcement that Tom planned to run for county attorney following his retirement, the dancing began.

Partnered by Dale because she couldn't get out of it without hurting his parents' feelings, Kyra continued to be tormented by jealousy. She was compelled to endure Dale stepping on her toes with almost every move he made while David led Suzy around the floor with smoldering, attentive grace.

They're lovers, she thought in anguish, forced to remember what it had been like to move in his arms. And everyone in the room knows it. Can't they wait until he takes her home before having at each other? It didn't occur to her that David had always danced that way, no matter who his partner was. Or that he wasn't looking particularly pleased with himself.

At last she'd had all she could take. Excusing herself, she headed for the ladies' room, only to dart out again when she overheard sandbox chitchat about David and Suzy coming from several of the stalls. To her relief, a different ladies' room on the opposite side of the bar turned out to be deserted. She was able to hide out there for a few minutes in peace and pull herself together.

Despite her efforts, she was still looking a little grim as she headed back toward the party through the bar, navigating in her spike heels between its deserted, miniature dance floor and the rust-colored club chairs that surrounded a half dozen tables. Intent on maintaining some semblance of indifference, she didn't notice the tall, dark-haired man in evening clothes who was lounging against the bar until he reached for her arm.

To her astonishment, David had abandoned his date and escaped for a solitary beer.

"I thought you'd gone," he said, a world of surprise and pleasure in his deep, husky voice. "Stay. Have a drink with me. We ought to talk."

Chapter Three

The moment spun out, gossamer thin, brimming with possibilities, yet as easily ravaged as a spider's web, tentatively connecting them. *What about your date?* she longed to ask. *Won't she be miffed if she finds us with our heads together?*

If she refused his invitation, or turned it into an occasion for sarcasm, she would never know what he wanted to talk to her about. Or if he'd have offered some explanation for walking out on her. The ache in her heart might continue to fester.

Deciding to accept, she slid onto the stool next to his and placed her small faille clutch purse on top of the bar. When he retook his seat, their knees were almost touching.

"What would you like?" he asked in the soft, deep voice that had figured in so many of her dreams. "A margarita?"

He'd fixed margaritas for them in the shabby trailer he'd called home when he was working for her father.

Having barely touched her champagne during the bevy of toasts that had been drunk to honor Big Jim's forty years of service, Kyra thought it would be all right to indulge. "Sounds good," she agreed, the toe of her left shoe accidentally brushing his trouser hem as she crossed her legs.

Storing away the small, inadvertent intimacy, he ordered, remembering precisely how she liked her tequila and lime concoctions—with just a dash of triple sec. He gave her a chance to taste the drink's tart coolness before initiating any further conversation.

"Ironic, isn't it, that we've met again because of another Naminga case?" he said at last, holding her captive with his light, unreadable gaze. "Did you hear what happened to Leonard in prison?"

It wasn't the tack she'd expected him to take. Apprehensively she shook her head. Well aware of the kind of atrocities that took place in prisons, she wasn't sure she wanted to hear the answer.

"He was gang-raped," David supplied. "He no longer speaks."

"How horrible!" she whispered, briefly shutting her eyes. "Poor, *poor* Leonard. He didn't deserve to be locked up like that...let alone what happened to him in that awful place. He must be so confused, so deeply humiliated..."

Her compassion for others, particularly the fragile and downtrodden, was one of the things that had always attracted him to her. In his opinion, she had boundless heart for a *gringa*—more than most people he'd met.

"Promise me that if you begin to think Paul could be innocent, you'll help me uncover the truth," he requested.

"Of course," she said. "Dad would do the same."

The answer was too glib, too easily proffered. He wanted her word. Short of that, there'd be no basis for them to start afresh. It would be difficult enough to reach common ground, he realized, given the way he'd walked out on her five years earlier, without a word of explanation.

"I'm not asking him. I'm asking you," he said, wondering how and when she would let him apologize. If he could make her see that he'd done what he had partly for her sake...

She was silent a moment, absorbing the remarkable force of his will, which was trained on her like a laser. Instead of explaining, or saying he was sorry, he was making demands. Incredibly she was inclined to give him what he wanted.

"Okay, I promise," she said. "It's the right thing to do, after all. Satisfied?"

His mouth curved in the ironic half smile she remembered. "It would take a lot more than that to satisfy me, White Shell Woman," he said.

It was another one of the love names he'd used for her, and she cringed a little, even as the endearment sank like rain into the soul place where she longed for him. Just to be near him again, to hear his voice and catch the downward sweep of his lashes when he was marshaling an argument or reserving comment, was a kind of apotheosis for her.

She couldn't let him waltz back into her life without explaining his actions and making amends, the way someone might walk into a house they'd trashed and abandoned, nonchalantly reclaiming it. Or talk about sex as if it were a possibility for them. Unfortunately for her resolve, everything about him was still perfect, exactly the way she liked it, from his air of compressed energy to the graceful half-moons of his fingernails.

"I don't think..." she began.

A familiar voice, originating in the hall that led to the room where Big Jim's party was still in progress, interrupted them. "There's been a five-car accident on the interstate west of town and Red has to leave," Flossie Miner said, glancing from her to David and back again. "I just wanted to say good-night. Call me in the morning, darling, if you have a chance."

"Will do," Kyra promised, dreading the well-meaning questions she was likely to face.

After Flossie left, she had to get back to the party before she and David became an item and her effectiveness in helping her father was seriously compromised. Kyra told herself she hoped she wasn't retreating out of cowardice.

It's not the time or the place to set things straight, thought David, though his heart was eager for that. We need a chance to be alone, without distractions or interruptions. Accordingly, he didn't argue when she said that perhaps she'd better be getting back. It was her father's special evening, after all. She belonged with him.

Still, he was too determined to have her after all the time they'd spent apart to let her completely off the hook. She was about to get to her feet when, suddenly, he reached across the space between them to cover her hands with his.

"You've probably heard I have a ranch north of town, on Route 89 near the San Francisco Peaks," he said. "My name's on the mailbox. Come anytime. I'll show you around."

Riding home the short distance that separated the country club from her father's house in his Lincoln Town Car, Kyra listened with half an ear to his running commentary about who'd said what and to his retelling of several of the jokes she'd missed.

"Several people told me they saw you sitting in the bar, playing patty-fingers with David," Big Jim said, changing the subject as they pulled into the drive and he raised the garage door with a flick of his automatic opener. "Say it isn't so."

"I stopped to talk with him for a few minutes, if that's what you mean," she admitted. "I could hardly avoid it. He was sitting there when I walked through on my way back from the rest room."

Her father was silent for a moment as he drove into the garage and switched off the engine. Then he said, "I hope he wasn't trying to quiz you about the Naminga case. Or get back in your good graces."

Though David had mentioned Paul, he hadn't asked her for any information he could use—his by right, or otherwise. As for her good graces, it would take a lot for him to storm the moat that protected *them*.

It occurred to her that acceptance of him and surrender weren't that far apart. He wants to go to bed with me, she acknowledged with a little shiver of anticipation. Complete the conquest my scruples denied him. And he's laying the groundwork.

"Don't worry, Dad," she fibbed. "I'm immune to his charms. As for Paul's case, we didn't really discuss it. He did mention Leonard Naminga and the fact that he'd been raped in prison. I suppose this is as good a time as any to ask if you could use your influence to help him win parole."

To Kyra's surprise she fell asleep that night the moment her head hit the pillow. She wasn't to be so fortunate in escaping thoughts of David the following day, however, as she set about reinterviewing the prosecution's key witnesses. Everything about the reservation's arid moonscape reminded her of him, as she drove from Flagstaff to Moenkopi to talk with the young girl who'd seen a man in Paul's costume enter Ben Monongye's dressing room trailer.

David grew up out here, she thought, poor as mud, no doubt imbibing a sense of wrong done by the white man along with the beans, cornmeal mush and watered-down coffee that were his daily fare as a child. Maybe his reason for leaving me was as simple as the fact that he didn't want to get married and I was holding out for that. Maybe the money my father offered him seemed like recompense for the hardships he'd endured...a kind of well-deserved bonus.

Whatever his motives had been, he would be pleased to learn that she'd continued to ask the question she'd posed to Julie outside the jail, namely, "Did anyone besides Paul want Ben Monongye dead?" And begun to compose a list of the Hopi construction company owner's enemies, if only for her own reference.

She wasn't terribly surprised when some of the same names kept cropping up. Feeling more like an independent investigator than a member of the prosecution team, she justified the path she was taking by reminding herself that her father was sworn to seek justice, no matter what form it took.

That night, the Miners, Marie Johnson—also a neighbor—and the Cargills, along with their son, Dale, were scheduled to arrive at her father's house for dinner and an evening of bridge, beginning around 6 p.m. Though it was to be an informal affair, Big Jim's part-time housekeeper had been engaged to cook for them.

Given the fact that she'd probably draw Dale for a bridge partner, Kyra was far from heartbroken when he failed to show up on time and the meal started without him. Maybe she would get lucky and he wouldn't come at all, she thought. Her father and his friends could play hearts, or something.

To her chagrin, he phoned as the roast beef was being served, to let them know he hadn't mixed up the date. She was privileged to take the call.

"A problem came up at one of my construction sites," he said, his somewhat nasal twang faintly slurred as if he'd downed a couple of stiff drinks on the job. "Feel free to start without me. I'll be there as soon as I can make it."

I can't say I'm looking forward to it, Kyra thought, as she gave her father the message.

Grateful the table talk didn't revolve around her renewed acquaintance with David and the history of their relationship, Kyra murmured whatever responses she deemed necessary as she pushed her food around on her plate without really paying strict attention. However, one item of gossip caught her interest. It arose as part of a discussion of the latest Washington, D.C., scandal, in which yet another senator had resigned, hoisted by the petard of his salacious and ill-advised personal diary.

"I'll confess...I'm surprised anyone would bother to jot down the details of daily life nowadays, what with all the obligations everyone has," Big Jim remarked. "Let alone use their diary as a confessional."

Betty Cargill differed with him. "Lots of people keep diaries," she said. "I always have. So has Dale. He probably picked it up from me. Though he's hardly the literary type, while I'm a former English teacher, he's kept one faithfully since high school. As for using them as confessionals, they're therapeutic."

Hoping to duck out when the meal was finished and leave the card-playing to her elders, Kyra stifled her disappointment when Dale arrived as dessert was being served. It didn't take much coaxing on Big Jim's part to talk him into having roast beef and mashed potatoes first, thus prolonging the agony. She was forced to watch him shovel food into his mouth as she helped the housekeeper pick up the plates while Red Miner and her dad set up the card tables.

Gradually the thought of being Dale's partner—having to put up with his clumsy flirting, dull conversation and ineptness at cards for an entire evening—became too much for her and an escape plan took root. What I want is to see David, she thought. That's all I care about.

She just wasn't sure she had the guts to take him up on his invitation. It was entirely possible that, if she drove out to his house without warning, she'd find that Suzy Horvath had beaten her to the punch.

There was only one way to find out.

"Dad...everybody...I'm developing a nasty headache, probably from poring over court files and driving out to the rez," she said, employing the local epithet for reservation, "to talk to witnesses without my sunglasses." She massaged her temples for emphasis. "If it wouldn't be too detrimental to your fun, I'd like to opt out of cards tonight...take a drive instead. A little fresh air might help."

Before Dale could try to talk her out of it or offer to come along, the Miners begged off, too. "Red was out at that accident scene until 3 a.m.," Flossie said. "And, like a fool, I waited up for him. We really aren't up to counting trump this evening."

Giving Flossie a grateful look while avoiding her father's unspoken questions, Kyra snatched up her purse, a cardigan sweater that matched her pullover and her car keys. You're probably crazy to do this, she chastised herself as she got into the Cherokee and headed northeast on her way out of town. Nothing good can come of it.

At the same time Kyra was heading out the door, David received a call from Suzy Horvath. "I know it's a little late to call with an invitation, but have you eaten yet?" she asked, when he answered on the first ring. "If not, what

do you say I pick up a bottle of wine and some steaks…
come out and cook for you?''

Briefly silent, David admitted to himself that, before
Kyra had come back into his life, he'd probably have taken
her up on it. "Not tonight," he answered, declining to add
a word of explanation.

Her voice betrayed disappointment, incipient jealousy.
"Sure I can't tempt you?" she persisted, her bright,
friendly manner failing to hide her urgency.

Though he hated to hurt her feelings, his answer was
unequivocal. "Sorry. But I have other plans."

After hanging up the receiver, David headed back to the
island range top in his cozy wood, stone and copper kitchen
in order to add some seasoning to the slow-cooked Navajo
lamb stew he was making. He wondered if those plans he'd
referred to would be realized. The worst that could happen
was that he would dine alone, he guessed. In view of his
mood, it was probably his second-best option.

He was probably mad to expect that on the strength of
a casual, nonspecific invitation, Kyra would materialize.
Yet as he'd removed the lamb chunks from the freezer after
finishing his day's work, he'd had her in mind. Wanting
her there, in his house, had become an obsession from the
day Jody Ann Daniels had informed him she'd be helping
her father with Paul's case.

In a way, this house was built for her, he acknowledged,
though he'd never really thought she would set foot in it.
He got out the ingredients for the corn dumplings that
would steam to delicious tenderness atop the bubbling, aromatic stew his grandmother, Mary Many Horses, had
taught him to make.

He, who had balked at marriage when she'd been so
eager to wear his wedding ring, had built her a house. If
she was everything he remembered, everything he'd

dreamed about, he would beg her to wear it now, given half a chance. First, he knew, he'd have to set things straight—plead with her to forgive his young man's lust for freedom and selfishness.

Arranging the bowl of fresh corn kernels and the dry ingredients on the counter, he decided not to mix them with the butter and milk yet. First, he'd wait a little. Learn to believe in miracles. Though it was getting on toward eight-thirty, it wasn't too late for her to darken his doorstep.

As she drove northward on Route 89, which seemed a lot less familiar after dark, Kyra was having second thoughts. What an idiot you are for taking his casual remark so seriously, she reproached herself. At the very least, you could have waited a few days...gotten more specific directions. He's going to think you're still crazy about him.

Vacillating between the image of a warm welcome and the painful realization that he might already have female company, she squinted into the darkness, trying to read the names printed on the country mailboxes that were planted next to the occasional dirt or gravel track that wound away from the highway, disappearing among the trees. Everything in her wanted to turn and run, give up danger for the known safety of her unhappiness.

In response, the risk taker in her experienced a stab of fatalism. If she could find his mailbox in the dark, she'd knock on his door. It was that simple. The decision was out of her hands. I don't need to come up with an excuse for visiting him, even to myself, she thought. I'm simply taking him up on his invitation out of curiosity, not agreeing to forgive and forget his mistreatment.

To win back her esteem or even a fraction of it, he'd have to confess to taking the money without being asked. And he might not realize it was a prerequisite. It was conceivable he hadn't guessed her father had told her about the bribe he'd taken, she thought. That her father would have been willing to admit the part he'd played in it.

However things worked out, she didn't have to fall in love with him again. If she kept her wits about her, she could indulge her curiosity about the way he lived, now that he was a success, and walk out when it was satisfied, with her chin up.

Slowing down a little more, she was able to locate his mailbox. With a fluttery feeling in the pit of her stomach that was part fear of making a big mistake and part wild, unexpurgated hope, she turned left on the gravel track beside it and lurched between piñon- and juniper-studded pastures, past a corral and well-built horse barn to higher ground, a stand of ponderosas and his magnificent house.

It appeared that he was home. There were lights in several windows.

Parking the Cherokee in his gravel turnaround, Kyra got out and closed the door on the driver's side sufficiently to switch off the interior lights without slamming it. Nervously she smoothed her hair and her tan wool slacks. If he was listening to music as he sometimes did, he might not have heard her arrival. There was still time, enough time to turn tail and go. Even as she contemplated it, she could feel the pull of his proximity and her corresponding yearning.

I want him to admit what he did, she soothed herself, lifting his door knocker and rapping it against heavy paneled wood. To say it was the biggest mistake of his life and that he thoroughly regrets making it. If he can do that, maybe I can throw off the shackles of the past and get on with my life.

Of course, once the Naminga case was over, she'd be going back to her job in Kansas City. As much as she'd always dreamed of making love to him, she wouldn't be foolish enough to get that involved.

Though she'd summoned him with her knocking, she jumped back a little when he opened the door and stood gazing down at her with pleasure and something like gratification in his beautiful eyes.

"Come in," he said after a moment, stepping aside for her to enter. "Dinner will be ready in twenty minutes or so. I've been expecting you."

Chapter Four

She'd eaten very little at her father's dinner table, barely picking at the main course and passing up dessert. Now, suddenly, she was ravenous as she caught a whiff of the delicious aroma that was wafting from his kitchen.

"Something smells wonderful," she acknowledged, filling up the silence that rested between them.

The attractive lines beside his mouth deepened. Having her there, in his house, instead of just imagining it, gave him the most amazing sense of completeness. It's as if the heart of my home has been lacking, he thought. And her coming has supplied it. Mentally, he hummed a line from his tribe's hogan building chant. *Happiness is poised to fall into place, ni yo o.*

"Lamb stew, Navajo style, with corn dumplings, plus a small salad. Canyon de Chelly peach cobbler for dessert," he said aloud. "A friend from Chinle brought the peaches when he visited last week. You always did like to eat."

Being around him gave her an appetite, and not just for things edible. She couldn't seem to keep from staring at

the way his faded jeans hugged his narrow hips and his
frayed corduroy shirt strained a little over his shoulders
from too many washings. Compared to their low-key sen-
suality and comfort, her sharply creased wool slacks and
ivory cashmere twinset seemed a little too dressed up, even
affected.

At least tonight I didn't put my hair up in a chignon, she
consoled herself, knowing he liked it loose. Several times,
when they'd been working together on the Leonard Naminga case, they'd come close to having sex. On at least
one of those occasions, when she'd lain atop his magnificent body on his trailer's lumpy single bed, kissing him
into a state of delirium, he'd confessed how much he liked
her curtain of hair hanging about his face.

"It's like a waterfall," he'd whispered.

If only he'd wanted her enough to send her father packing.

With a start, she realized he was watching her succumb
to might-have-beens, and she quickly switched to an inspection of her surroundings. From what she could see of
the living room, with its oversize stone fireplace, comfortable sofas upholstered in chocolate piqué-velvet and terra-
cotta, Mexican tile floors softened by glowing red and
brown Navajo rugs, his house had been designed and decorated with exquisite taste.

His surprisingly varied collection of Native American
sculpture, pottery and basketry rubbed shoulders comfort-
ably with a few African pieces and a three-quarters of life-
size, nineteenth-century primitive, cigar store Indian. A
modern, pop art painting of an Apache warrior in reds,
browns and yellows dominated another stone wall, which
intersected at a right angle with the fireplace.

Everywhere she looked, she saw attention to simple,
soul-satisfying comfort—a fire neatly laid with aromatic

hardwood, a Navajo blanket in earth-and-dusk tones slung over a chair for wrapping up in on a cool evening.

"I'll be glad to give you the grand tour," he offered with a little smile at her obvious curiosity and approval, "just as soon as I mix up the dumplings and drop them in the stew to cook."

In response to his light touch at the small of her back, she preceded him into the kitchen to perch on one of the bar stools that surrounded his freestanding island counter, topped by a copper hood.

She'd always liked the way he moved, and it was pleasant just to sit there, watching his efficient, matter-of-fact execution of traditional feminine chores, despite the serious bones she had to pick with him. To her way of thinking, his culinary expertise only emphasized his masculinity. It called to mind the knack he'd always had with preparing and seasoning food, even when *posole* and beans had been best suited to his budget.

With the dumplings made and the temperature of his stainless-steel wall oven turned down so the cobbler wouldn't burn, he opened a chilled California chardonnay. "Grown by a friend of mine, whom I defended in a civil suit," he remarked, pouring out two balloon-shaped glasses of the pale gold wine and handing one to her.

Accepting it, Kyra hoped he wouldn't propose a toast. Something along the lines of "to the good old days" would plunge them from an uneasy truce into indictments and recriminations. And she didn't want that, yet.

He seemed to sense it. "Let's save the toasts for later, shall we? And have a look around?" he suggested.

Wineglasses in hand, they trekked to his office first. Reached from the kitchen by a long corridor that effectively separated it from the rest of the house, it was in reality a minioffice complex, with a room for his secretary, another for him, plus a half bath and space for storage.

I'll have to build on a room for her, if I can talk her into becoming my partner in every way possible, he thought, watching her face as she inspected his personal work area with its shelves of law books, mission-style desk and broad wall of windows that looked toward the night-shrouded peaks. He knew there'd be a lot of hard-scrabble riding between the talus-slope of wishing and the butte crest of fulfillment and not much time in which to do it, just the few short weeks she'd set aside to hang around Flag and help her father with his case.

For himself, he needed to know her again—be sure at the gut level that his clamorous instincts were on target. Yet on a spiritual plane, he trusted them.

He had to be right for her, too, of course. If he could get her to see that he'd been ripe for Big Jim's picking when the wily county attorney had suggested he bow out for her sake, both financial and academic, maybe she'd forgive him for avoiding a painful explanation. They could begin again, slowly and blissfully winning each other.

Next came the dining room, which formed the house's second cluster in conjunction with the living room and kitchen, where he paused to check on his culinary creations. Relatively modest in size, the dining room was marked by a continuation of the living room's stone walls and a sweep of sliding glass doors overlooking the patio and swimming pool.

The table and sideboard had been fashioned of honey-toned ash. There was just one painting, a luminous oil in turquoise, gold and faded scarlet against a taupe background depicting a dancer at one of the Hopi ceremonies.

"I love your collection of baskets," Kyra said, gently touching one of the light-and-dark patterned Papago,

Apache and Navajo woven vessels that were arranged atop his sideboard. "I'm probably a little crazy. But, to me, baskets as special as these have more significance than containers for berries or cornmeal. They seem to invite fantasies about the past, and create space for possibilities...."

It was his feeling exactly. There must be Native American blood in the Frakes clan's history, David thought. Or maybe on her mother's side. There was just time for him to take her through the bedroom cluster before their meal would be ready. "C'mon...I'll show you where I sleep, and then we can eat," he suggested, attempting to keep his words free of seductive undertones.

Though his offbeat dwelling had sung to her, body and soul, since she'd walked in the front door, it was his bedroom that caused Kyra to emit a little sigh of longing to inhabit such a place. Built in a more avant-garde style than the rest of the house, it was roughly oval in shape. The ceiling soared to twice the height of the other rooms like the canopy of a contemporary glass-and-cedar cathedral, toward a skylight that admitted the sun and stars.

Smaller than the one in the living room but generous nonetheless, a stone fireplace buttressed the airy construction on one side. There was very little furniture—mainly an antique chest for clothing and the bed, which consisted of a king-size mattress laid directly on the tiles and covered by a hand-pieced quilt.

Though it looked as if it could have been designed by some latter-day Le Corbusier, the room as a whole reminded her in some mystical fashion of the impoverished hogan where he'd grown up, with blankets placed on a hard dirt floor for sleeping and a fire hole overhead that let in the night air as it allowed cooking and heating smoke to escape.

He sensed she'd made the connection. "You can take

the boy out of the rez, but you can't take the rez out of the boy,'' he said wryly.

I wouldn't change a thing about him save one, she thought, aware that wishing couldn't undo past events. Meanwhile, the imagined splendor of what it would be like to sleep with him there, tangled up in a bronze-and-cream mosaic of limbs after wild and sustained lovemaking, had her by the throat.

Her heartbeat settled into a more normal rhythm as he ushered her back in the kitchen and they loaded the food on trays in order to eat outside by the pool. She felt cared for, even cosseted, as she nibbled at her salad and tucked away one delicious bite after another of his tender, redolent stew and corn-studded dumplings by the light of flickering hurricane lamps.

Avoiding the events that had surrounded their breakup, their conversation revolved around her work in Kansas City and several of his more recent high-profile cases. After a while, David brought up the subject of his mother's great-grandfather and personal mentor, Henry Many Horses, who'd died in the brush arbor outside his hogan on the banks of the Little Colorado several years earlier at the ripe old age of ninety-one.

"I remember meeting him once," Kyra said. "He was a medicine man, wasn't he?"

David nodded. "When he was young, his specialty was curing ceremonies, and he followed them to the letter of Dineh tradition. As he grew older, though, he began to look beyond the prescribed rites to incorporate some of the esoteric teaching his grandfather had bequeathed to *him*. Gradually he developed what he described to me as 'the extraordinary powers all people possess to move beyond time and space, in order to get at the truth.' When he knew he wouldn't be around much longer, he passed those secrets on to me, so I could follow in his footsteps.''

Kyra wasn't sure she understood. Whatever the significance of his mother's great-grandfather's teachings, she doubted David would give up his satisfying and remunerative law practice to become a tribal medicine man. All she knew was that he seemed to radiate a new confidence and quiet assurance. He was not quite as brash or determined to ride roughshod over everyone in order to get what he wanted.

They had coffee with the cobbler and dollops of rich vanilla ice cream to finish. "No cigar?" she asked when he didn't light up before piling their dirty dishes back on a tray.

He shook his head. "That was a young man's affectation. I've grown up a little since then."

They listened to a compact disc of R. Carlos Nakai playing the flute as they did up the dishes. From what David could tell, the wronged, still-seething woman who'd wrenched free of his embrace in the courthouse lobby the day before was nowhere in evidence. However, he didn't doubt that she'd emerge if he looked at Kyra crosswise or took an awkward step.

When they finished, he showed her some photographs he'd taken for a book he hoped to complete someday about the influence of traditional dwelling places on the architecture favored by some successful, modern-day Americans of Native descent. Surprisingly, he'd run into a number of houses during his travels throughout the West that paralleled his own in that respect.

Unknown to her, he was marking time, waiting for the customary hour of digestion to pass before proposing a swim. If he could talk her into taking a dip in his pool before she brought up the subject of leaving, they might have a few more hours together.

When finally he put forward the idea, she gaped at him in surprise and consternation. "It's fairly cool outside," she protested. "Or hadn't you noticed? Besides, you can't possibly imagine that I brought a suit."

He'd have to soft-pedal his arguments if he didn't want them to backfire. "Actually, the pool's heated," he pointed out. "If we keep our shoulders under the water, we'll be warm enough. As for a suit, you don't need one. If you have scruples about swimming nude, I can switch off the lights. There's a new moon tonight, so it's exceptionally dark. I have an extra robe you can wear to keep warm when you're not in the water."

Going along with his casual yet highly provocative proposal would be just begging for trouble, she knew. Yet she'd begun to think it was exactly the kind of trouble she wanted. Despite the hurt and anger she still felt, the sensuous woman in her was clamoring for it. As she mulled over the idea, the lovestruck girl who'd suffered a broken heart at his hands held her breath.

You're not a virgin anymore, she decided, allowing herself to be talked into it. If he catches a glimpse of you without your clothes, it won't be the end of the world. The fact was, she'd been dreaming of him for years. Though it was ill-advised and more than a little dangerous for her sanity, she wanted to indulge the part of her that still yearned for him.

"Okay," she conceded with a shrug to cloak her excitement. "I suppose it wouldn't hurt."

Their hands brushed as he handed her the white terry cloth robe he'd promised her, evoking lost possibilities. I wonder if he's sorry that he made the choice he did five years ago, Kyra thought. However he feels about it, he can hardly expect to take up where we left off. I'll swim with him to show him I'm my own person now, that I'm not afraid of succumbing to his wiles. And then I'll go. When we meet again, it'll be as courtroom adversaries.

Taking off her clothes in his guest bath and putting on her borrowed robe, she accompanied him outside. In deference to her, he was wearing a similar garment. She watched with a little shiver of excitement and nervousness as he switched off the golden glow of the patio lamps, followed by the underwater lighting system.

Everything went black at his touch, rocketing into an unfamiliar world of shadowed shapes and night bird calls beneath the zillion or so stars that peppered the velvety Arizona sky. I'm really here, Kyra thought in amazement. With *David*. We're really going to do this.

Seconds later she heard a splash. Letting his robe fall silently on the flagstones that surrounded the pool, the man she couldn't seem to get out from under her skin had slipped naked into the water.

"C'mon in," he invited, surfacing. "After the first little shock, it's really quite pleasant."

Though she couldn't see him well, she could make out the shape of his shoulders, the glint of his eyes and his sleeked-back hair.

"Turn around and I will," she offered.

He complied at once, facing away from her toward the mountains that held sacred significance for his people. He hadn't promised not to *imagine* how she looked, though, with her pink, upturned nipples and the sweet curve of her hips exposed to the cool night air. Or to dream of parting the triangle of blond curls that nestled between her thighs and exploring her feminine mysteries. And he indulged himself to the fullest in that pursuit.

Several smaller splashes and a wave of ripples alerted

him she was in the pool. He could feel her gasp at the water's chill, which would quickly pass as she adjusted to its temperature.

He'd had the pool built extralong, for laps. "What do you say we swim to the deep end to warm up?" he suggested.

At her murmur of assent, they took off with lazy, parallel strokes. Only their mutual presence in the water connected them. But it was enough to set their fantasies ablaze.

If he tries to touch me, I'll get out of the pool, dress and drive like hell for Flagstaff, Kyra vowed—even if that means he'll get more than a glimpse of me in the buff. Yet she had to admit a wet, impassioned embrace that linked past and present in an arc of feeling was exactly what she craved.

Their fingers brushed again as they reached the pool's opposite end and she took hold of the apron. Though their shoulders remained beneath the water's surface, their bodies were inches apart. Her mouth was close enough to his that his breath seemed to float against it.

"Warmer now?" he asked, a helpless tone creeping into his raspy-soft voice.

"Some," she admitted.

Was he going to kiss her? Her principles wouldn't see daylight if they embraced in that wet, naked state. They'd become lovers and then enemies, if they didn't tackle the past's power to hurt them.

It took all the self-control David possessed to keep from enfolding her. He'd wanted her so badly, for so long. Every nerve ending in his body was aching for it.

I'll be damned if I'll seduce her for the sake of a night's pleasure, only to lose all her tomorrows, he thought, a muscle twitching alongside his jaw as he willed his arousal to subside. If she's ever to give me another chance, I'll have to take it slow. Gentle her like an abused filly. Prove that things are different.

Abruptly detaching himself from the intimacy of their tête-à-tête, he pushed off against the side of the pool and swam with brisk, athletic strokes to the shallow end. As Kyra watched, confounded by his sudden withdrawal, he mounted the shallow steps to the pool decking and retrieved his terry robe.

The imperfect glimpse she got of his dripping, bronze nakedness before he fastened the robe about his waist only made her lust for him more. You should go home, she told herself. Place yourself beyond the reach of temptation, before you do something rash.

"I believe I'll get out, too. Could you, um, turn your back?" she requested, striking out for the shallow end as well.

He didn't want to look away. And in the end he didn't. Silently begging her to understand that a man can exercise just so much restraint, he held out her borrowed terry cloth wrap.

She could see he was simply going to watch. If she begged or threatened to get him to turn his back, she guessed he'd change his mind. But she didn't want to resort to that. Let him look, she decided. And eat his heart out. A regular jogger who worked out at a gym near her Kansas City condo three times a week to release some of her physical tensions, she was in the kind of shape that would cause lost opportunity to look awfully damn sweet.

She'd tempt him briefly and announce that she was leaving. Rising up out of the water with liquid grace, she didn't allow her gaze to waver despite the downward flicker of his eyes. Or the mute praise they contained when he raised them.

The night air striking her wet body attenuated her tri-

umph as, thrusting her arms into the robe he held out to
her, she was overcome with a paroxysm of shivers.

"Ah, baby..." Ashamed of his arrogance in insisting she
show herself to him, David put both arms around her.
"Come over to one of the lounge chairs and let me warm
you," he begged. "I'll build a fire for us."

Her feeling of being cared for winning out over the desire for vengeance, Kyra gave herself in to his keeping. She
allowed him to settle her on one of the double-wide chaises
and tuck a soft, somewhat worn Indian blanket around her.

When he lit them, the twisted, aromatic piñon branches
he'd stacked in a conical arrangement atop his adobe "fireplace" caught instantly, causing flames to leap up from
what was really just a round, hoodless platform for logs,
open to the stars. There was very little breeze and, within
moments, she could feel the heat.

Returning to her side, David put one arm around her—
more friend than would-be despoiler. "Better?" he asked.

She nodded. Though his solicitous behavior might be just
so much courtroom drama or the prelude to a seduction,
she wasn't going anyplace.

"I had the fire cradle built for just such an evening as
this," he said, neglecting to add that he'd pictured her beside it while it was still on the drawing board. "When I'm
home, and it's warm enough, I often spend the night out
here, under the stars."

Kyra promised herself she wouldn't do that, recalling his
penchant for camping with just a bedroll. But she would
stay for a little while. "Living in Kansas City, I forgot how
clear the sky can be," she murmured. "The constellations
seem close enough to touch. Like the Pleiades. What was
it you used to call them?"

She could feel him smile that she'd remembered a little
of what he'd taught her. *"Dilyehe,"* he answered. "My

Navajo forebears, who were mostly hunters and gatherers before they turned to raising sheep, did what little planting and reaping they carried out by their movements.''

"You once told me a story...."

"About how the heavens were populated with a bag of crystals?"

"That's the one."

"It tells of the order in which Black God set the stars in their places—Man with Feet Ajar, Horned Rattler, Thunder, The Rabbit Tracks.'' He used the Navajo names. "But his meticulous care in arranging things wasn't to go unchallenged. Coyote, the Trickster, snatched his bag away and flung its remaining contents to the four corners of the universe, creating the vast, nameless-to-the-Navajo-stargazer brilliance of the Milky Way.''

By now, Kyra was feeling warm and comfortable. "That's a pretty story,'' she said with a yawn. "Someday, if you settle down and have a family, you'll have to tell it to your children."

He wanted to give her babies—with greater intensity each moment they were together. Any children they made would represent the best of both cultures, he thought. They'd be tawny and perfect as they emerged from her beautiful body.

They had a long way to go before he could speak of why he'd left her and expect her to understand his reasons. If he tried to bring them up too soon, she'd fling them back in his face.

"You know," he said, changing the subject slightly, "some of the ancients who studied the sky believed, like quantum physicists today, that all moments in time exist simultaneously. My great-grandfather agreed with that theory. He claimed humans can travel to the past...even step forward in time if they achieve the necessary wisdom and the need is great enough.''

When Kyra didn't comment, he asked if she thought such feats were possible.

''No offense to your great-grandfather. But I really don't,'' she admitted. Yet she was keenly aware that David's personal power and magnetism had increased a hundredfold since they'd worked together on the Leonard Naminga case. According to him, the old man had passed on secrets. ''You're not saying *you* think them to be possible, are you?'' she asked.

His answer was noncommittal. ''Why would I do that,'' he teased, ''when you've warned me you wouldn't take it seriously?''

Disengaging himself after a bit, he got to his feet again and put several more pieces of wood on the fire. Though it offered the perfect chance to announce her departure, Kyra didn't utter a peep.

I don't want to go yet, she admitted, despite the way he sold me out five years ago. Maybe that's because I never learned to stop wanting him. If I can indulge myself now, without succumbing, maybe I can return to Kansas City with the missing pieces of my heart back in place.

That it was probably a vain hope, given the strength of her feelings for him, didn't bear thinking about. Like a lemming rushing to self-destruction, she didn't object when, with the fire stoked to suit him, David returned to her side and drew her close. All she could think about, as his cheek rested against her hair, and her lips were pressed to the sweet-smelling warmth of his neck, was that they were really there, together.

Chapter Five

The fire was so warm. The air so cool by contrast. And his arms so sheltering. Without intending it, Kyra drifted off to sleep to dream of a billion stars looking down as David's great-grandfather wove their names into a Navajo legend-in-the-making.

A very different scene greeted her when she awoke. For one thing, it was already daylight. Somewhere a horse whinnied as a man called out training commands. Someone else was operating a piece of heavy equipment, possibly a mower of some sort.

With a start, Kyra realized that David's half of the padded chaise they'd shared was empty. Meanwhile, she was still in her borrowed robe with nothing beneath it. Her clothes, her purse and the keys to the Cherokee were somewhere inside his house. They'd spent the night together, she thought incredulously. Her father must be beside himself.

She was working up her courage to go inside and retrieve her belongings when David slid open one of the patio doors and stepped outside bearing a mug of coffee. Unlike her, he was fully dressed in a clean pair of faded jeans, a black buckskin shirt and a pair of cowboy boots. Clearly having showered and shaved, he looked like a man who'd already spent considerable time at his desk.

"Hello, sleepyhead," he said, holding out the steaming pottery mug to her with a glint of amusement in his eyes. "I'll go easy on the narcoleptic jokes until you've had your morning fix."

She made a face. "Thanks a lot. I can't tell you how much I appreciate it."

The coffee was strong, black and hot—the way she liked it. She decided to take several restorative sips before attempting to undo what she considered to be the damage she'd done by spending the night with him.

"My housekeeper's here, cooking breakfast," he added before she had a chance to speak. "Soon as you're fully awake, we can go inside and eat."

Kyra stifled a groan. What must the woman think of her, camping out all night with David—in one of his bathrobes, yet? It was safe to say she hadn't formed a very wholesome impression. Of course, she might be used to overnight female visitors. The phenomenon might be commonplace.

Aside from seeing each other in the buff, nothing untoward had happened. They hadn't even kissed. Compromising as it might look to the casual observer, she could hold her head up.

"I feel a little silly, falling asleep out here instead of heading home where I belong," she murmured, realizing too late that it sounded like an attempt to vindicate herself.

"Don't give it another thought," he replied. "The air out here will do anyone in, especially if they're not used to it."

He's probably right, she realized. I've spent too much

time poring over law books and interviewing witnesses during the past few years and too little hanging out in a place I love, if a dose of fresh Arizona air is enough to undermine my scruples. Unfortunately, moving back to Flagstaff with him so close isn't an option.

The glint of amusement intensified. "So...are you going to come in and have breakfast with me of your own free will?" he demanded. "Or do I have to carry you?"

Each time she agreed to go along with one of his schemes, she was taking another step down a very slippery slope. Yet in this instance she didn't seem to have much choice. Refusing his hospitality after letting him make dinner for her and, later, spending the night on his patio would be the height of grumpiness.

"Thanks, but I can probably make it under my own steam," she answered, getting to her feet and cinching her borrowed robe more firmly about her waist.

David's graying, sixtyish housekeeper, whom he introduced as Margaret Yazzie, a distant cousin, was a person with marked Navajo features and quiet dignity. She was just sliding an omelette stuffed with mushrooms, goat cheese and mild chili peppers from her blackened skillet onto a glazed terra-cotta platter.

"Hello," she said shyly, her downcast eyes strongly suggesting that overnight female guests weren't a run-of-the-mill affair insofar as she was concerned. "Do you want melon with your eggs? Or orange juice?"

Kyra asked for melon. As they ate on bar stools positioned at one end of his island counter, David advanced the first of two proposals he had in mind.

"I know it's unorthodox. But I'd really like you to talk to Paul Naminga," he said offhandedly, hastening to add at the look of rejection on her face, "I don't expect you to change sides. Or do anything that would compromise your father's case unless the idea originates with you. It's just that I'm so strongly convinced that Paul's innocent..."

If he is, Kyra thought, my father, Red Miner and the grand jury have made a colossal mistake. She was silent a moment. "You mean...you'll let me talk to him alone?"

He shook his head. "As his attorney, I have to be there. But I'll stay in the background...call a halt only if I think he's about to say something that isn't in his best interest."

That seemed reasonable enough. It was his duty as Paul's attorney to keep the Hopi paramedic from sinking his own case. Meanwhile she viewed the opportunity he was offering her as an interesting, possibly useful one. She doubted her father would see it that way. If she knew him, he'd be thinking in terms of preventing a mistrial based on prosecutorial misconduct.

"I might consider doing it," she answered finally. "I'll have to let you know."

When at last they couldn't eat another bite, David advanced his second proposal—a suggestion that they meet at the scene of Ben Monongye's murder for a quick look around before separating to go about the day's business.

"Though I was on the museum grounds during the festival, I didn't see the fight," he said. "I was in the stands, watching the show, which had been going on for around ten minutes, when Red Miner took over the microphone and made the announcement. Pandemonium broke out. I'd like to walk around the area and review what happened without a mob looking over my shoulder...check out how much time it takes to move between a couple of points. Since you weren't there...didn't even see the festival setup, it might benefit you to do likewise. I'll be glad to point out where the trailers, stage and bleachers were situated."

The way he's acting, we're a couple of cops investigating a murder with no known perpetrator, she thought. Of course, that's his job as defense attorney. But it isn't mine. If I'm not careful, he and Julie Naminga will have co-opted my loyalties without offering me any hard evidence of Paul's innocence. And my dad will have another reason to be furious. Yet she had to admit she'd wanted to check out the scene, too—get it straight in her head.

She could wash up in his guest bath, she supposed. Have a proper shower and change of clothes when she reached her father's house. "Okay...I'll follow you to the museum grounds," she agreed at last. "But I can't stay long. I may be twenty-seven years old and thoroughly emancipated. But Dad doesn't see it that way. He still worries over me as if I were a teenager. Given the fact that I didn't return home last night, he's going to be on the warpath."

In fact, I'm not sure how I'm going to explain it to him when I can't fully account for it myself, she realized as she put on the slacks and sweater that, fortunately, she'd placed neatly on wooden hangers in his guest room closet the night before. She'd been suffering from a kind of compulsion to be around David, she supposed. To see how he lived, et cetera, as a kind of antidote for all those years of wanting him.

On their way to the museum grounds, during which David led in the pickup truck he used as a ranch vehicle and Kyra followed in her Cherokee, David kept asking himself if he was trusting her too much. The rest of Paul Naminga's life was at stake and the Hopi paramedic was counting on his attorney to defend him. He'd be derelict in his duty if he helped Kyra turn up even a speck of evidence that bolstered the prosecution's case.

What I *really* want is for us to form a team to dig out the truth, the way we tried to do before, and have her fall in love with me again, he thought.

He doubted it would be that simple, though. The great

unasked—and unanswered—question of why he'd left her without any explanation stood in the way. Only instinct had kept him from trying to tackle it yet. Though she wasn't as tense as she'd been when she'd walked into her father's office, or as antagonistic as when he'd kissed her in the courthouse lobby, he realized that one wrong move would blow his chances.

The kiss had been a mistake, no matter how much he'd yearned for it. Since forcing it on her, he'd been trying to win her over with low-key friendliness, despite an instinct for more passionate arguments.

When they reached the museum grounds, they parked in the regular lot and walked around the building to the tire-rutted field behind it where the dance festival had taken place. Stakes with bits of yellow crime-scene tape still clinging to them had been driven into the ground by Red Miner's deputies, marking the former positions of the grandstands, the stage and the trailers used as dressing rooms by Paul and Ben, respectively.

"Paul and Ben weren't the only ones to use those trailers, were they?" Kyra asked when David had finished pointing out the various stakes' significance.

He shook his head. "They were just the *last*. According to Suzy Horvath, who organized the affair, at least forty-five dancers were scheduled to perform. There were four trailers available for dressing. That makes eleven or twelve people using each trailer if everybody showed. As you might expect, Red Miner had the trailer where the murder took place roped off as soon as Ben's body was discovered. To my mind, that imbues the unidentified hairs his crime-scene detail turned up with a little more significance. When you add them to the fact that they found no hairs belonging to Paul or any of the other dancers, no fingerprints..."

He let the observation dangle as he pointed out the area

that had been occupied by craft booths, food stalls and portable toilets. "Additional parking for the festival was roped off over there," he said, pointing to the far side of the field, which abutted a little creek.

"Where was it the boys were supposedly hanging out to sniff glue?" Kyra asked.

He pointed to a grove of cottonwoods that fringed the creek, now in yellowing leaf. "I calculate it would take a man in good physical condition maybe a minute and a half to run each way at top speed, weaving between the cars over uneven terrain," he said, "plus at least three or four minutes to check out the kid who passed out. That makes roughly five and a half minutes...enough time for someone else to slip into Paul's costume and kill Ben, then return the costume to Paul's trailer unnoticed."

"Maybe...if nobody was around," Kyra answered. "Unfortunately for your theory, there were quite a few people milling about."

David shook his head. "You're forgetting that both he and Ben were very late getting dressed. The horn alerting the dancers to report to the stage and the audience to be seated had already sounded by the time a few stragglers among the festival-goers put a stop to their fisticuffs."

Kyra was still looking skeptical. "If Paul's innocent, it's pretty hard to believe that nobody saw anything that would exonerate him, with literally hundreds of people on the grounds," she said.

"Someone did, remember? That young girl, who noticed a *Koyemsi* going into Ben's trailer around the time Paul says he was tending to the boys. If I can find those boys and they can place the time as well as corroborate his story, your dad will have to look for another suspect. I agree, whoever the murderer was—and I don't believe for one minute that it was Paul—had to be a little crazy to try something like that. It meant taking an awful risk.''

He was doing his best to inculcate doubts about her father's case. Maybe that's what this whole game plan of his was all about, she thought. All this restraint and nurturing and friendliness was an effort to win her over to helping him. When a straightforward assault on her senses didn't do it, he decided to take a more subtle approach. Beneath all the depth and wisdom he seemed to have acquired, she decided, he was the same old David, playing her as skillfully as R. Carlos Nakai played the flute, to get what he wanted.

Not this time, she vowed. I have experience on my side. And some fairly graphic memories of what his abandonment cost me in emotional terms.

"Thanks for showing me around. And for dinner last night. I'd better be going before my dad sends out a posse to search for me," she said lightly, getting out her keys and hitching her shoulder bag more firmly on her shoulder.

He responded by walking her back to the Cherokee.

"When am I going to see you again?" he asked softly as she got behind the wheel.

Imagining a note of insecurity in his husky, deep voice had to be utter foolishness. The last thing he'd *ever* been was insecure. "As you know, I came to Flagstaff to help my dad," she reminded him with a little shrug. "It stands to reason that I'll be spending most of my time with him."

David didn't know how to answer her. He wondered if it was something he'd said. Or done. One minute she'd seemed friendly, if somewhat guarded, the next as fractious as a filly about to balk. Mistrust and a sudden eagerness to be gone had stared back at him from her big green eyes. Her capacity to forgive and love him again seemed a thousand miles distant.

He was brooding, off center as he waved goodbye to her and returned to the area where the rented trailers had been parked on the day of the festival. Approaching the spot where Paul and Ben had come to blows, he stood quietly, his head bent and his arms hanging loosely at his sides, seeking to tune out the screech of a hawk that was circling overhead and the distant murmur of traffic on Route 189, as well as his longing to mend things with the woman he wanted.

As he saw them, his great-grandfather's instructions for stepping through one of the "gaps" or "openings" into the past that existed wherever the aura of significant human emotion lingered were both uncomplicated and profound. To accomplish it, you had to shed all attachment to the personal consequences of what you could learn, while retaining your desire to uncover the truth, and step through the open gap when its glimmer invited you. When it involved a case he was handling, he had to care for his client's sake, instead of his growing reputation.

Though the modest formula had worked for him more than a dozen times since he'd learned it, and he tried repeatedly that morning, he couldn't generate a ripple of past-relatedness in the seamless morning light.

It's Kyra, he realized, letting his concentration go slack. I'm too focused on her. I want to know who the real killer is, not just because the truth could set Paul free, though that's certainly the case, but because I want to impress her with my integrity and my brilliance.

Giving himself a moment's respite from trying, along with a mental shake to loosen up his metaphysical "muscles," he gave it another whirl. The result was the same. Like most of his contemporaries, who'd never learned the principles of journeying between time layers at an elder's knee, he was firmly stuck in the present until he could summon a disinterested ego state.

That could take quite a while, he guessed.

I may as well phone Sister Margaretta, he thought, remembering that he was supposed to check back with the Catholic nun he'd once assisted by defending one of her protegées without charge. Maybe she had come up with something.

At his request a week or so after the murder, Sister Margaretta had promised to ask around at the Native American school where she taught near Kayenta, on the reservation, in an attempt to learn the name of the boy who'd summoned Paul to help his glue-sniffing friend, as well as those of his fellow miscreants. It was possible one or more of the school's students had been involved, as a busload of them had traveled to the festival.

Still nursing his discouragement, he dialed her number on his cellular phone. And hit pay dirt. "David...I'm so glad you called!" she exclaimed. "I was just going to ask for permission to phone you. The boy who summoned your client for help on the day of the murder may have been one of our students. Though he won't admit it to me, several of his classmates said he described the situation to them in detail. He won't want to repeat it for your benefit, of course. I know it's quite a drive out here. But maybe if you talked to him..."

To Kyra's dismay, Big Jim hadn't gone to his office as usual that morning. Instead, when she walked in the front door of the house where she'd lived as a teenager, he was pacing the living room with one eye on the clock and the other on the telephone.

"Kyra, for God's sake!" he shouted when she bade him a tentative hello. "Where've you *been?* I was afraid you'd gotten in an accident. Or met with foul play. That your body would be found in a ditch or something! Dammit, gal... I was on the verge of asking Red Miner to send out his deputies..."

I should have known better than to think my private business would stay private around here, she thought, flushing to her hair's natural blond roots. No matter if I'm twenty-seven years old. As long as my father's alive, I'll be his little girl, incapable of taking care of myself. Or making my own choices.

"I'm glad you didn't, Dad," she answered with as little irritation as she could manage. "Because it would have fairly embarrassing for us both. You see, I spent the night at David Yazzie's house...."

An angry flood of invective drowned out any attempt she might have made to offer an explanation. "When I asked you down here to help, I never dreamed you'd get mixed up with him again!" Big Jim bellowed, his muddy brown eyes flashing with anger behind his wire-rimmed spectacles as he ran one chunky hand through his thinning, sandy hair. "The fact is, I thought you had more sense. After the way he—"

"Left me with a ten-thousand-dollar bribe from you in his pocket?"

Her father had the grace to look abashed. "I thought you forgave me for my part in that mess a long time ago, sweetheart," he said after a moment.

Her arms were around him in an instant. "I did, Dad. I did. At least *you* had my best interests at heart. But I didn't forgive David...especially not for taking the money. You don't have to lose any sleep over my staying at his house. We didn't become intimate. After what he did to me, I wouldn't have sex with him if he were the last man on earth."

Relief spread over his face like butter melting on a pancake, though she had the oddest sense there was something furtive, almost guilty about what he felt.

"Well, I'm glad to hear that, at least," he muttered.

"I needed to tie up some loose ends where he was concerned, that's all," she added, attempting to offer a rationale for behavior she couldn't fully explain to herself.

Seemingly mollified, her father took umbrage all over again when she told him David had offered her a chance to talk to his client and she was considering taking him up on it.

"He's going to sweet-talk you into working for the defense, just see if he doesn't," he predicted, "though I asked you down here to help, not hinder me in getting a conviction. It'll be like a replay of the Leonard Naminga situation, with you and David on his side and me on the other. Well, don't say I didn't warn you. The only loyalty David Yazzie knows is to his own kind. Once he wins an acquittal, he'll toss you aside like yesterday's newspaper."

In Kyra's opinion, the reference to David's "own kind," which seemed to suggest that he'd do whatever it took, legal or otherwise, to win acquittal for a fellow Native American, was deeply fraught with prejudice. But then she'd always known, deep down, that her father abhorred the idea of a Navajo son-in-law, despite his much-vaunted liberality in hiring David half a decade earlier.

"David Yazzie's not going to co-opt me for the defense without my say-so," she insisted. "But you ought to realize one thing... I'm not going to help you prosecute Paul Naminga if I decide he's innocent. I told David you'd feel the same way...that the truth mattered to you just as much. The way I see it, only good can come from me talking to Paul. Whether he's innocent or guilty, I might learn something."

In the end, Kyra's dad gave his grudging permission for the meeting to take place. Shortly afterward, he left for his office. Alone in the house, as his housekeeper had gone into town to shop for groceries, she found herself struggling with guilt and a million uncertainties as she scrubbed with bath gel and a loofah mitt beneath her shower's cleansing spray.

Her stewing over the matter was abruptly short-circuited by the shrilling of the telephone. Trailing water on the bedroom carpet, she managed to answer on the third ring.

"Hi," David's voice rumbled in her ear. "I've got a lead on the boy who summoned Paul to help his friend on the day of the murder. According to a friend of mine, who teaches there, he boards at the Catholic mission school near Kayenta. How would you like to have lunch, see Paul and, afterward, drive out to the school with me?"

Still dripping, Kyra pulled the towel she'd snatched up more tightly around her body. He wasn't giving her a moment to draw breath.

"I suppose I should warn you," he added when she didn't say anything. "It's quite a drive. And I won't want to head back immediately if there's any chance to interview the other boys, as well."

It sounded as if the jaunt he was proposing could turn out to be another overnight affair. If she agreed to go and failed to return again that evening, her father would be apoplectic.

Balancing that prospect was the pleasure she couldn't seem to help taking in hearing David's voice. His suggestion that they check out his lead together seemed to pour balm into all the hurt places where she'd yearned for him.

You'd be crazy to fall in love with him all over again, she warned herself. Your Dad's right...all this attention on his part is probably just a scheme to undermine the prosecution's case.

She didn't want to believe it. The Kyra who had sworn to uphold justice as a profession was champing at the bit, while the spurned young woman she'd been was begging for sufficient time in his company to wring an apology from him. For some reason the conversation she'd had with her dad, particularly the guilt trip he'd laid on her, was pushing her in the same direction.

"Well?" David asked finally when she didn't answer his question.

"Forget lunch," she answered decisively, making up her mind in an instant. "I can have a sandwich here. I'll meet you at the jail around one o'clock. We can play it by ear from there."

She wasn't all that surprised when nothing new came up during their conversation with Paul Naminga. She reflected that if the Hopi paramedic was innocent, he probably didn't have anything else to tell, whereas a guilty man would be sending up a smokescreen of misinformation. A little drawn, from several weeks of living behind bars spent contemplating the ordeal he faced, Paul seemed essentially as she'd pictured him—honest, soft-spoken, a man who put his wife and seven-month-old son first and foremost.

Though she had no proof, she emerged from the interview all but convinced of his innocence. If that's the outcome David wanted, he got it, she thought. Despite what I told Dad, I'm ready to switch sides if we turn up the smallest piece of corroborating evidence.

It occurred to her that if they were to spend the night on the reservation, it might look better to Big Jim—and David—if it came about by accident. "Tell you what," she said as they left the jail. "I'll drive the Cherokee as far as

Gray Mountain Trading Post. That way, if you have to bring me back tonight and head back east, you won't have so far to go.''

David gave her an appraising look, his head tilted slightly to one side. Had she misunderstood the caveat he'd issued that morning? If so, he decided, he wouldn't call her on it.

"Whatever you're comfortable with," he said after a moment. "We can play it by ear, the way you suggested."

Chapter Six

A stiff wind was kicking up as Kyra parked the Cherokee next to David's pickup in front of Gray Mountain Trading Post and its small, adjacent post office.

"Get in quick! There's a dust devil about to hit," David warned, reaching across the pickup's cab to open the door on the passenger side.

Snatching up her oversize shoulder tote and flipping the Cherokee's automatic locks, she was beside him in an instant. Their denim-clad knees touched briefly as she closed the door and he stuffed the tote behind the seat. The possibility that he'd kiss her hovered between them, nascent and tremulous.

With effort, David managed to suppress the urge. Seconds later, the dust devil struck, a bantam-size whirlwind of grit, sand and stray twigs that would have stung her face and hands without inflicting serious injury if she hadn't sought shelter promptly enough. Surrounding them like a miniature tornado, it swirled against the windows and beat a tattoo on the truck's metal surfaces.

Seconds later it was gone, taking with it some of the tension it had created. "Let's go," David murmured, shifting into Reverse. "We have a lot of ground to cover."

Kayenta was roughly a hundred miles distant.

On her drive to Flagstaff from Kansas City, Kyra had crossed the ancestral lands set aside for the Laguna and Acoma peoples of New Mexico, but she had only skirted the vast Navajo nation that spread across portions of three states, surrounding the much smaller Hopi enclave.

Immersing herself in it now brought back memories of the past she and David shared. When they crossed Route 64, which peeled off to the left toward the Little Colorado River Gorge, she couldn't keep herself from glancing in that direction. Several times during his courtship of her, five years earlier, they'd gone that way to visit his great-grandfather and his grandmother, Mary Many Horses, whose wood and tar paper shack was situated near the gorge's rim.

"Grandmother asks after you every now and then," David said, throwing her a quick glance. "If you'd like, we can visit her one of these days."

I'd like, Kyra acknowledged silently. She'd always felt a strong affinity for the lean, weathered woman with wiry, gray hair and snapping dark eyes who'd given up sheepherding in her seventies to earn a precarious living selling cheap jewelry to the infrequent tourists who passed her humble dwelling on their way to the Grand Canyon. She was also extremely fond of the gorge itself. A scaled-down version of its better-known cousin with the same pink, sienna and ocher rock walls and a sandy, cottonwood-fringed river bottom, the Little Colorado lacked the Grand Canyon's seven-thousand-foot-plus elevation. Barren-looking grazing land surrounded it instead of pine forest.

As they continued on their way, patches of green against

the almost uniform brown of the landscape became increasingly rare except for the straggly cottonwoods that lined dry washes, cutting across an arid moonscape. Though they passed several families of reservation dwellers headed for town with children, and the occasional grandmother in traditional dress, relegated to their trucks' open beds, they saw few sheep ranchers on horseback—just an occasional boy or elderly man on foot, hurrying after his flock. After a while, to fill the silence that seemed to flow from the bleak vistas that surrounded them as much as from their unshared thoughts, David turned on the radio.

They reached the school at Kayenta around 4 p.m. The pace of an after-class game of kickball slowed to a near standstill as the group of junior high boys playing it paused to watch them get out of the truck and head for the administration office.

The school's principal, Father Andrew Ward, was expecting them. "Come in, come in," he said, his face creasing in a smile as he removed his wire-rimmed spectacles. "You're always welcome here, Mr. Yazzie. We're very grateful, you know, for the sporting equipment you donated last month, not to mention those math and history books...."

Brushing aside what promised to be a litany of thanks with a deprecatory gesture, David introduced Kyra as a "friend and colleague." "I trust Sister Margaretta told you the purpose of our visit," he said, pulling out a chair for Kyra before taking a seat.

"She did, indeed." Picking up the phone on his battered desk, the school principal dialed an extension and said a few words into the receiver. "She'll be here with Tom Tsosie in just a minute," he said. "I think it only fair to warn you...he's refused to say a word about the incident. Or even to acknowledge that it took place."

David and Kyra exchanged a glance. On their way to the school from Flagstaff, he'd predicted as much.

A moment later Sister Margaretta and her charge appeared. Skinny, gangling, dressed in threadbare sweatpants and a frayed T-shirt with an unruly lock of poker-straight dark hair falling forward into his face, Tom Tsosie appeared to recognize David. "Who's she?" he asked, jerking his head in Kyra's direction.

David's voice was reassuring, nonjudgmental. "A friend who's interested in seeing justice done," he answered. "I represent Paul Naminga, a Hopi paramedic who performed at the Flagstaff festival. As you probably know, he's been accused of stabbing a fellow dancer to death. I have reason to believe you can account for part of his time that afternoon...help back up his alibi."

Belligerence flashed in the boy's eyes. "Why would I want to do that...to help a *Hopi?*" he demanded. "My uncle had to move his sheep to a worse grazing place when the government increased their holdings. Besides, I don't know nothin', anyway."

Though David tried several more times, patiently emphasizing that without his testimony, an innocent man might have to spend many years in prison where he'd be at the mercy of thugs and perverts, the answer was the same. Tom Tsosie hadn't sought out Paul or asked for his help. He and his friends had smoked a few cigarettes. That was all. No, he wouldn't give the defense attorney their names. It would amount to ratting on them.

At last Father Ward gave them a helpless shrug. "I'm sorry to say that many of our students have an underdeveloped sense of their Christian and civic duty," he said regretfully.

With a glance at him, Sister Margaretta whispered something in David's ear.

"Sister is suggesting that Tom and I might speak alone in the courtyard outside the chapel," he said promptly. "Man to man."

Though it was clear that he believed the exercise would be a futile one, the principal gave his permission readily enough. Watching from one of his office windows as David strolled with the defiant youngster between dusty cottonwoods and a few stunted rosebushes that had been planted beside a dry adobe fountain, Kyra thought she could detect a gradual softening of the boy's demeanor.

His manner deferential in a way that appeared to blunt the strength of his persistence, David could be seen to elicit some answers. Before long, Tom Tsosie seemed to be talking freely with him. He made a number of what looked like explanatory gestures.

After some twenty minutes or so of intense conversation, David shook hands with the boy in what was clearly an expression of thanks. Following a few words of gratitude to Father Ward and Sister Margaretta, he was ready to depart.

"I gather he told you everything you wanted to know," Kyra said as they bade the principal and Sister Margaretta goodbye and got back into his pickup truck. "How'd you manage it?"

David gave her a look. "I told him a little more about Leonard and what happened to him behind bars," he said. "That he wouldn't have been brutalized that way if there'd been a witness to stand up for him. Fleshing out the story with a name and some of the more telling details made a difference, I guess. After thinking it over and struggling with his conscience, Tom confirmed Paul's story."

She didn't answer, and for a moment his strong, beautiful hands rested indecisively on the steering wheel. "The boy who passed out was a good friend of his," he continued at last. "He lives with his grandmother in a remote settlement between Rough Rock and Chinle Wash. It's a fairly isolated spot. The last few miles of roads are practically nonexistent. It goes without saying that they don't have a telephone. We won't be able to call them first."

Though it would be dark in another hour, he was hoping she'd agree to accompany him.

"What are we waiting for?" she asked.

Giving her a brief hug of appreciation, he started the pickup's engine. The hug had left her yearning for more and she ordered herself to be sensible.

By the time they spotted the thin plume of smoke that arose from Ruby Nez's hogan, which nestled beneath a frowning mesa, night had overrun the landscape. Feeling bruised and shaken from the gauntlet of dirt tracks they'd been forced to run to reach their destination, Kyra wondered why David didn't get out of the truck and knock, or call out to alert the owner of their presence.

"When you live in a place where the silence is this great, you can hear visitors approaching from many miles away," he explained in answer to her unasked question. "Besides, Navajo manners forbid anything so brash and discourteous as demanding entrance to another's residence. Ruby Nez knows we're here. If she's willing to see us, she'll let us know."

Following a wait of what seemed like six or seven minutes, but in reality was only two or three, a slight, gray-haired woman who wore her scanty braids in traditional squash-blossom pinwheels on the sides of her head appeared in the hogan's doorway and motioned to them.

Indicating that Kyra should follow him, David got out of the truck and approached. "Forgive our intrusion, Mrs. Nez," he said respectfully. "I'm David Yazzie, Paul Naminga's lawyer. This is my friend, Kyra Martin. Am I right in thinking you've heard about the murder that took place at the Flagstaff dance festival?''

Ruby Nez nodded, her weathered face betraying little or no emotion. "My grandson, Wilson, is inside," she said. "You're welcome to come in and talk to him."

She knows, Kyra thought in amazement as she followed David into the low, one-room dwelling, which was warmed by a small fire of brush and twigs in the central fire pit. When he sat, she sat cross-legged beside him on some piled-up blankets. Either the boy had confided in his grandmother, or she'd found out via the grapevine, with no telephone and what must be few visitors in this isolated place.

A moment later thirteen-year-old Wilson Nez stepped out of the shadows, clearly unhappy at having been run to ground but well aware without a word being spoken that his grandmother required his cooperation. Apparently an ingrained deference to her authority took precedence over his fear of punishment for his behavior at the Flagstaff festival and disinclination to get involved. After a show of reluctance that was met with frowns of disapproval from her, the truth came tumbling out. Without being asked, Kyra took down the most salient points of his testimony in a pocket-size notebook.

It had all happened as Paul Naminga had claimed. Wilson, Tom Tsosie and several other friends had been sniffing glue in an attempt to "get high" while their elders attended the dance performance. Abruptly becoming light-headed, Wilson had passed out, hitting his head on a protruding tree root. When he'd regained consciousness, the Hopi paramedic had been leaning over him.

"Did he advise you to see a doctor? Or stop by an emergency clinic to be checked?" David asked.

The boy nodded.

"But you didn't, did you?"

"I didn't want to get in trouble."

"Any idea what time it was when Paul headed back toward the festival area?"

"Uh-uh. I ain't got a watch."

Without a fairly accurate reading of *when* the events that corroborated Paul's story had taken place, they wouldn't fully exonerate him. Though the window of opportunity would have been tight, he'd still have had sufficient time to revive Wilson Nez, change into his *Koyemsi* costume, fatally stab Ben Monongye and join his fellow dancers onstage as if nothing out of the ordinary had occurred.

Meanwhile, it was 9:17 p.m. They'd had no evening meal. They were many miles from Flagstaff, in one of the most remote parts of the reservation.

"I have some distant relatives near here who would give us some supper and a place to sleep," David submitted, inserting his key in the truck's ignition without turning it.

Kyra didn't want to be indebted to him or his people, or find herself trapped with relatives who thought he could do no wrong. Yet they were both clearly too exhausted to make it back to Flagstaff without pushing themselves to the limit.

"If you don't mind, I'd rather not impose on your family," she answered, beginning to think of the disappointment and irritation with which her father would probably greet their day's handiwork. "Don't you know of a place where we can have a bite of dinner…maybe rent a couple of motel rooms for the night?"

His expression devoid of any clue to what he was thinking, David considered her proposal. "There's a fairly decent motel on Route 191, near Chinle, forty miles or so from here," he said after a moment. "Last time I looked, there was a restaurant next door. If it stays open late, we might be able to get a bowl of chili or something.''

Without any response from her, he headed in that direction.

As they bumped and lurched over the uneven dirt track that had led them to Ruby Nez's front door, Kyra leaned against the door frame on the passenger side. Forgetting the progress they'd made in exonerating Paul Naminga and the renewed confrontation with her father that was probably inevitable, she let the past wash over her.

She'd been devastated when, following Leonard Naminga's conviction five years earlier, David had walked out of her life without a word, leaving her father to explain the collusion that had prompted his departure. If it hadn't been for the anger that had surged in her to take its place, the sense of betrayal she'd felt might have tempted her to drop out of law school. Only sheer grit and a fierce, almost manic determination to show David Yazzie that she'd be fine without him had driven her to finish, with grades that were impressive enough to win her a slot in the Office of the U.S. Attorney.

Now I'm getting mixed up with him again, she thought. And for what? If I insist it's solely to help Paul, to do what I can to see that the truth comes out, I'm kidding myself.

She might have a recurring dream of making love to him. But she'd never want to marry him now. Or become intimate. Lacking an apology and an explanation of his actions that she could accept, she didn't trust him enough.

Her stomach was beginning to growl by the time they reached the motel, which huddled with a gas station and the little café he'd mentioned at a bend in the narrow, black-topped highway. To her dismay, though the motel's Vacancy sign was lit, the café's old-fashioned exhortation to Eat had gone dark. Its doors and windows were tightly shuttered.

"What are we going to do?" Kyra asked plaintively. "I'm starved."

David was kicking himself that he hadn't stopped to pick up something earlier while there'd been time. Or he could have insisted that they stay with his relatives. But it was too late to backtrack to those solutions. A quick count of the assorted vehicles parked in front of the motel's single-window cabins warned him that they'd better move quickly if they wanted a place to lay their heads.

"Maybe we ought to check in before somebody else comes along and snatches up the last remaining rooms," he suggested. "Afterward, I can get us some junk food and sodas from the station's vending machine."

It would have to do. Getting out of the truck, Kyra accompanied him into the motel office.

"We'd like two rooms for the night, if you have them," David told the bored-looking manager, who'd been munching on a greasy, microwaved burrito as he watched a wrestling match on the snowy screen of his antiquated television set.

"Only got one," the man replied. "With twin beds. The price is twenty dollars a night. I'm about to close up. Take it or leave it."

With a glance at Kyra, who acquiesced with a faint, incredulous nod, David filled out the registration form and held out his hand for the key.

Highly conscious of his proximity and the fact that they would be spending yet another night together, Kyra stood awkwardly by while he unlocked the door to their temporary abode. It proved to be spartan in the extreme, its furnishings limited to a shabby desk and chair, a nonfunctioning portable TV and two lumpy twin beds that were separated by four feet or so of space. In sleep, they'd be almost close enough to touch.

"Why don't you take your shower while I run over to the gas station for our 'dinner'?" David suggested, attempting to ease the awkwardness she clearly felt. "All I ask is that you save me a towel."

Despite the dinginess of the cramped shower stall, which contained a number of broken tiles, it felt good to wash off the dust that clung to her skin from the day's journey. Fortunately she carried a toothbrush and miniature tube of toothpaste in her leather tote, so she was able to care for her teeth as well.

Thanks to her unwillingness to admit, even to herself, that they'd been headed for another night together, she'd deliberately neglected to tuck pajamas or a nightgown into her capacious purse. Looks like I'll have to sleep in the T-shirt I layered under my sweater, and my bikini underpants, she thought, uncomfortably aware of how tantalizing those skimpy garments were likely to prove. Maybe if I can manage to slip under the covers before he returns...

She heard him come in as she was towel drying her hair. Having stripped off his shirt, he was sitting naked to the waist on the bed closest to the window when she emerged, pulling off his cowboy boots. The ripple of his arm and chest muscles beneath the smooth envelope of his coppery skin as he renewed the effort was a stirring sight.

"What booty I could come up with is on the desk," he said, casually gesturing toward the cache of chips, candy bars and cans of soda he'd placed on its top for her inspection.

All his real attention was focused like a laser on the incredibly delicious way she looked in her lace-trimmed panties and thin cotton T-shirt. He'd always been wild about her small, round buttocks—so perfectly shaped for a man to squeeze. As for the shadowed smudges of her nipples, the memory of how they'd stood upright at just a touch of his fingertips had his arousal pumping and his heart racing.

Though she selected a can of lemon-lime soda and a bag of nachos from the desktop, she didn't open either one. Instead she lifted the receiver on the phone that stood atop the room's single night table. "There isn't any dial tone," she announced.

"Want to call your dad...let him know where we are?" David asked, getting to his feet and pulling his cellular phone from his hip pocket.

They were standing very close in the narrow space. Having considered contacting her dad, Kyra had thought better of it. Her carefully cultivated gift of gab notwithstanding, she couldn't think of a single reason he would accept for her being holed up with David Yazzie in the Red Rock Motel on the Navajo reservation.

"Thanks. But I've changed my mind," she answered. "The fact is, I'm a grown woman. I don't need to answer to anyone."

At that, his eyes took on their smoky look. "If you really mean it..." he said.

Seconds later he was tugging her into his arms and she was letting him, succumbing to her most profound feminine instincts as she spiraled deeper and deeper into the erotic wilderness of his embrace.

Chapter Seven

God knew, they'd kissed that way before, fiercely, precipitously, fused by a gravitational pull so strong it overcame all misgivings and objections, on fire with the need to be inside each other's skins, each other's clothing. Yet each sensed this coming together was different—so earth-shaking in compulsion and scope as to be unrecognizable at the root. The intensity of it seemed to rock the shabby little motel room, causing the floor, the threadbare carpeting, *their feet*, to lose purchase in the everyday world where actions and consequences rubbed shoulders.

They'd been apart—unthinkable!—too long, drowning in the same well of loneliness. During that time, she'd been initiated by someone she didn't love. And he'd worked day and night to fill the empty places, an essentially solitary man too frequently packing his bags and hitting the road as he fled the desert at his life's core.

If he could win her now...make her see that he'd make her a good husband, convince her to overlook his youthful sins...

"Kyra, my dove, my precious one," he said against her mouth, half-drunk with the unutterable sweetness of holding her again as his thumbs sought and teased the dark smudges of her nipples through the thin covering of her T-shirt.

Big with his craving for her, he was pressing against her portal. With his mouth mauling hers so tenderly, so heatedly, she couldn't think or protest.

"Kyra...Kyra...I've wanted you so much. Please forgive me for leaving you the way I did," he begged.

Yes...oh, *yes,* she thought, half-wild with what he was suggesting. What would it matter if I gave in, just this once? She could walk away whole, a woman who knew at last what splendor was, though she refused to settle for treachery.

Like the infamous thirty pieces of silver she'd learned about as a child in Sunday school, the ten thousand dollars he'd accepted from her father to leave her stood in the way. He wasn't going to admit to taking it. Or ask her pardon. Instead, he would disarm her scruples with his sex appeal.

Unless he tells me the full truth *without being asked* and apologizes from the heart, we don't have a snowball's chance in hell of fixing things, she thought, though I long to let him make love to me from the bottom of my heart.

Fleeting as water slipping over a stone, the moment shimmered and was lost. David could feel her withdraw from him—revoke her participation in spirit even before her hands pushed at his chest.

With a little twist of anguish on her face that let him glimpse the pain she felt, she turned away, toward the bed she'd assumed she'd occupy. Sitting down on it without renewing eye contact with him, she hugged her knees and stared at the blank television set, as if she expected to find an answer there.

Long, shapely and lightly tanned in the glow from the room's single incandescent bulb, her legs were incredibly beautiful. He ached to feel them wrapped around his waist, grasping him with all their strength.

"What's wrong?" he said with quiet reasonableness. "Why can't we kiss...explore a future together if it's what we both want?"

Her response was fast and furious. "Don't presume to tell me what I want!"

With a gesture that was calculated to hurt, she wiped her mouth with the back of her hand. "Could you possibly turn off that light?" she added. "I'm exhausted. I want to sleep."

She wanted to eradicate his taste. His scent. Well, he'd be damned if he'd let things end that way, now that they were together again. If she wanted to extract a litany of atonement for past hurts, he had no objection to reciting it. He'd do whatever penance was necessary, in any reasonable way she might suggest.

Flicking off the lamp, he plunged the room into darkness. For several seconds the only sounds in the room came from their breathing, the rasp of his zipper as he took off his jeans and the hurtling passage of a sixteen-wheeler on the highway outside their window. His bedsprings creaked in protest as he stretched out in his shorts and scrunched his thin, somewhat limp pillow into a makeshift support for his neck.

"Just because I haven't brought it up until now doesn't mean I don't know how wrong I was to walk out on you five years ago without a word of explanation," he said after a moment. "From the moment Jody Ann told me you were divorced, that you were coming back to Flagstaff to help your father, I wanted to clear the air. Apologize for hurting you. I haven't known how, or where to start."

Alone in the dark with him, marooned on the far side of the limitless chasm that separated their beds, Kyra let herself hope a little. Every word he spoke, every seemingly unrehearsed action he took made him appear strong and loving, innately decent. Yet in her heart of hearts, skepticism raged. What if he made a clean breast of everything and asked her forgiveness? Would she be able to give it? To trust him again? Without trust, they could never have anything together.

He'll have to bring up the money himself—admit to taking it, she decided. Maybe even repay Dad. I'm going to need that much.

"If it's any comfort, I've rued the consequences of what I did every day since," he added. "Not to defend myself, but by way of explanation, I was younger then...saddled with a backbreaking college debt over and above the help I'd received from the G.I. Bill. The fact is, I was damn near penniless.

"Despite the honor your father thought he'd conferred on me by hiring a Native American for his staff, I was making peon's wages. I wasn't ready or able to settle down...support a family if the need arose. I wanted the chance to get my feet wet as the kind of attorney I'd dreamed of being someday, maybe even earn a decent living in the process."

"You've certainly achieved your goals," Kyra agreed in a less-than-complimentary tone. "Ironically, being the man you are, you could have done it all with one hand tied behind your back. Why don't you just admit it? A wife and, God forbid, a baby would have cramped your style. You wanted sex without commitment...the freedom to walk away unencumbered whenever you chose."

It was a young man's sin and he'd been tarred by it.

Much as he'd wanted her, he hadn't wanted marriage—until it had been too late.

"You've got me there," he admitted. "I was immature. Self-centered. And self-indulgent. At the time I probably felt pretty much as you suggest. When your father came to me and said he was afraid you wouldn't finish your law degree if our affair continued, he seemed to be pointing to a way out that was best for both of us. I thought that, if I left...did what I needed to do with my life and gave you a chance to do the same with yours, we might find each other again when the time was right."

Rationalizing her pain, he'd turned his back on her, leaving her stunned and desperate. Now he wanted to come back, as if no grievous injury had taken place. "You've got to be kidding!" she exclaimed. "After you left without a word, and took..."

Somehow she managed to hold her tongue.

She hadn't managed to do it quickly enough. "What?" he demanded, the frown that drew his brows together an almost palpable thing. "Exactly what did I take?"

"My heart with you," she improvised, furious at the sappiness of her response and the necessity of sounding like such a victim in order to throw him off the scent.

It was his turn to mull over her words while remaining cloaked by the room's shadows. "How can that be, if you married someone else less than a year later?" he asked finally. "If it was love you felt, it didn't last long."

Was he accusing *her* of not caring enough?

"If you must know the truth, I married Brad Martin on the rebound," she said. "Like most unions of that sort, it ultimately didn't last."

The bastard had what I threw away...the chance to make you happy, David thought. And he blew it. "Look," he said. "If it makes you feel any better, there's never been anybody but you for me. I've missed you like part of myself every damn day we were apart. When I phoned you a week or so before you were set to graduate with your J.D., and got your roommate, I had an apology and a marriage proposal in mind.

"She told me you were marrying someone else. I could have tried to stop you, I guess. But I'd given up the right. Instead, I packed up my stuff and headed into the Little Colorado Gorge, to grieve. I probably stayed there, living off fry bread, berries and rabbit meat a good month."

If only I'd known! Kyra thought. I'd never have married Brad. Never have gone off on that disaster of a honeymoon with him. Yet what could she have done differently? Married David instead? The money he'd taken to dump her would have continued to stand in the way.

It did tonight.

"It doesn't matter anymore," she whispered.

"The hell it doesn't. We're still the same people, alive in the same world. I still love you every bit as much."

The words slipped like a dagger into her heart, their wound painful but bittersweet. Though she didn't answer, tears soaked her pillow.

His worst sin, he decided, had been to leave her without a word of explanation. Not for the first time he imagined her pounding on the door of his trailer, driving like a crazy person onto the reservation to learn his whereabouts. Several months after his departure, his grandmother had mentioned receiving a visit from her.

"Like a fool I bought into your dad's reasoning that if I stuck around long enough to say goodbye, you wouldn't let me go…that you'd drop out of school to be with me," he confessed. "He said we needed a clean break, one that would allow you to move ahead with your law degree and not look back. In retrospect I realize he probably didn't think I'd leave if I had to face you."

"But you would have. Wouldn't you?" Kyra said.

"Maybe not. In retrospect I think otherwise. How could I have, with your arms around my neck?"

A little shudder of emotion passed through her. "So... it's Dad's fault, then," she said, hiding it from him.

"I blame him less than I blame myself. I may not deserve it, babe. But I want to make a new start...say how sorry I am that I hurt you the way I did. I swear...if you can forgive my young man's selfishness and lack of judgment, you'll never have to suffer from them again."

Against her will, the flow of Kyra's tears intensified. Sweetly, with unbelievable humility, he was offering her what she wanted most. For five years going on six, the impossibility of ever having it had haunted her. Would that it *were* just selfishness and a youthful lack of judgment that stood between us, she thought. I'd fall into his arms with the force of an arrow speeding toward its target.

"It's not enough," she said, choking on the words.

Mutely he tried to read her thoughts across the gulf that separated them. Why had she stayed at his house last night and let herself fall asleep in his arms if she didn't want him? he asked himself. What was she doing on the rez with him now, at this very moment? "Tell me. What can I say or do to make things right?" he begged.

She'd vowed she wouldn't prompt him. But now she couldn't help herself. "You could admit to everything," she suggested.

His frown intensified. "I'm not sure what you mean. True, I've had a couple of affairs since we parted. And deeply regretted them. I thought they could make me forget you. But they only made the loneliness worse. I can't think of anything else that pertains. If you could just tell me what's on your mind...give me a clue..."

He isn't going to mention the money, she realized with a sinking heart. Let alone apologize for taking it. He doesn't guess I know anything of the sort ever took place. It probably hasn't crossed his mind that Dad would admit to offering it.

"Sorry," she persisted. "I want to hear it from your mouth first."

He was silent for a long time after that. She began to think that he'd gone to sleep.

Finally, "I've racked my brain, babe. And I'm not coming up with any answers," he said in a low voice. "If you won't tell me what's wrong, I can't make amends. What are we going to do about it?"

Her hopes in tatters, her soul still wounded, Kyra could only think of the hurt she felt. "The same thing we did before, I imagine...go our separate ways when the Naminga case is finished," she said bitterly, prompting a silence that was absolute.

Somehow she managed to fall into a troubled sleep. When she awoke, stirring at the dusty shaft of sunlight that had penetrated the room, David's bed was empty. Its thin coverlet had been neatly smoothed in place and tucked beneath his pillow. His jeans, shirt and boots were absent.

A quick glance in the bathroom revealed it to be empty of him. He's gone and left me stranded, Kyra surmised in panic, racing to the window and pulling back the short, somewhat grimy drape. To her relief, he was standing beside his truck in the clothes he'd worn the day before, talking on his cellular phone. Glancing up at her movement, he signaled that he'd be with her in a moment.

She'd better get dressed if she didn't want to parade in

front of him in her underwear. Hastily tugging on her jeans and pulling her sweater over her head, she stood before the bathroom mirror to smooth her disheveled hair and put on lipstick. She was still there, feathering on taupe and rose eye shadow with a little sponge, when he appeared in the doorway behind her.

God, but he's a beautiful man, she thought, staring at the reflection of his aquiline features, straight, dark hair and astonishing deep blue gaze. Despite the betrayal that tears at my heart, every instinct I possess argues for his decency, his essential goodness.

Could she possibly be mistaken about him? Seconds later, she decided that she couldn't. To believe him innocent was to brand her father a liar. Lifelong experience had taught her that deception wasn't part of Big Jim's makeup.

To her relief David didn't make any cracks about her putting on war paint, as he'd done once or twice in the past. Or tell her in his heart-stopping voice how lovely she was. Instead he simply stared at her face as if seeking some clue to the thoughts she'd refused to share with him.

When he didn't find any, his eyes took on a shuttered look. "If you're ready, I'll drive you back to Gray Mountain Trading Post," he said in a monotone. "There's a matter that requires my attention."

He was taking her at her word—accepting the rift she'd told him couldn't be mended and focusing on his work. To tell the truth, he seemed to be in a hurry. Adamant as she'd been that there could be no future for them, Kyra was deeply disappointed.

I don't want it to end this way, she admitted with a little thrust of panic as she snatched up her leather tote and followed him out to the truck. Yet I don't know how to keep that from happening. If I ask him about the money and he denies taking it, where will that leave us? I'll have to choose between believing him and believing my Dad. Though he'd made some major mistakes, notably bribing David to walk out on her, her father was still the most honest person in her universe.

Silence reigned most of the way back from the somewhat remote area of the reservation where they'd spent the night. Finally, in an attempt to annihilate it, David turned on the radio. The "love-gone-wrong" songs that were standard fare on the clearest, most powerful station he could find on his truck radio didn't help Kyra's mood much.

Famished after their mostly uneaten junk-food supper the night before, they paused briefly for coffee and pancakes at a little truck-stop restaurant in Tuba City, where some of David's fellow Navajos stared at the ivory-and-copper contrast they made as they sat across from each other, exchanging only the sparsest of sentences.

Too soon from her point of view, they were on their way again. It wasn't long before they were pulling in at Gray Mountain Trading Post.

"Well...this is it, I suppose," David said as she picked up her purse and started to get out of the truck. "See you in court."

She nodded. "See you."

He waited just long enough for her to start the Cherokee's engine before backing out with a splutter of gravel and heading back north, deeper into the rez. As she started toward Flagstaff with a heavy heart, Kyra wondered if he'd learned of a new witness he didn't plan to tell her about. If so, thanks to the rules of evidence, she and her father would hear about it soon enough.

Meanwhile, after talking to the boys they'd managed to interview the day before, she was anything but sure that Red Miner had arrested the right man. Unlike his brother, Leonard, Paul Naminga wasn't an alcoholic or mentally handicapped. Though it had been lacking in proof, his story had been articulate, plausible. Now, thanks to the corroboration they'd turned up, it was beginning to check out.

Happy as she was for Paul, Julie and their little boy that a ray of light had appeared at the end of that particular tunnel, she knew the Hopi paramedic wasn't home free yet. There was still the circumstantial evidence of the fight and the blood on the costume. They needed to find the real murderer.

A moment later she corrected herself. There could be no "they" involved in the search. *David* needed to find him. Or her. Thanks to their discussion in the little motel, which had driven the last nail in the coffin of their love, she and the part-Navajo defense attorney would never be a team again in any sense of the word. To face that, make herself believe it and gaze head-on into a future without him after tasting his kisses again, would be the toughest adjustment she'd ever have to make.

She was approaching the turnoff to David's ranch north of town when she realized with the certainty of inner knowing just where he'd headed. The mysterious "matter" that had so urgently required his attention had been a visit to his seventy-three-year-old grandmother, Mary Many Horses, in her hogan near the Little Colorado's rim. By turning east on Route 64 a few miles north of Gray Mountain, he'd pointed his truck directly at her place.

Though she'd showered the night before, she was wearing yesterday's clothes. Her hair needed shampooing. Common sense dictated that if she was going to be fool enough to turn around and go after him, she ought to go home and change clothes first. Maybe the quixotic, impractical notion would die aborning, saving her from herself before she put it into effect.

There wasn't time. She had to go now, before it was too

late. Without the slightest hope that he'd tell her the truth, even if she asked him. In her soul, which seemingly had become part Navajo and correspondingly spiritual in just a few days' association with the man she still loved, she *knew* it was imperative. If she didn't, she'd regret it to her dying breath.

On the moonscape stretch of reservation where he'd been raised, with its bone-dry grazing lands and stunning, half-hidden river canyon of rose and magenta and ocher rock, David was just pulling off the highway onto the dirt track that led to his grandmother's humble dwelling place.

As if she'd known he was coming and had calculated his arrival down to the second, she was standing outside her door, waiting for him to approach. A slight woman with long gray braids that reached most of the way to her waist, she was wearing the traditional dress she favored.

Halting his pickup a few feet away so she wouldn't have to breathe in the cloud of dust he'd generated, he turned off the engine and got out. "Grandmother," he said simply, allowing his pain to show in his face.

It didn't surprise him that she guessed its source. Or that her love and compassion surrounded him even before they touched.

"It's still Kyra, isn't it?" she asked. "Somebody told me she was back in Flagstaff."

He nodded helplessly. "She's divorced now. But she won't have me. I don't know what to do."

"Come inside," Mary said in her gentle way, resting one wrinkled hand on his muscled forearm. "We'll talk."

Seated on a blanket so old that its colors had faded until they seemed to blend visually with the hogan's beaten-earth floor, David poured out the secrets of his heart. He had a worthy client to defend. Yet, so far he'd been unable to discover the real murderer. Or come up with sufficient evidence to win the man's acquittal.

Simultaneously Kyra had returned still angry with him. Though she'd seemed to forget her mood long enough to spend the night at his house and accompany him to the reservation in search of some witnesses he sought, she'd turned on him the minute he'd tried to resolve things.

She seemed to want an apology that went further than the one he'd tendered for leaving her without saying goodbye that long-ago autumn morning. But she refused to be specific. For some unknown reason, the first mention of his unknown sin had to originate with him.

"I'm completely in the dark about what she wants," he confessed. "What I did was leave without telling her why, knowing how much it would hurt her. It was a bad thing to do. Callous. Cowardly. And insensitive. I've paid dearly, a hundred times over. In no other way have I knowingly given offense."

Mary Many Horses was silent for several minutes, considering what he'd told her. "Why haven't you spoken to Great-Grandfather Henry about this?" she said at last.

The question brought up another thorn that was pricking him. "The powers he taught me have weakened," he admitted. "Whenever I try to use them, they recede from my grasp."

Again silence filled the hogan as Mary closed her eyes, searching for correct guidance. At one point she muttered a half-vocalized prayer in the Navajo tongue.

"You must make a spirit pilgrimage into the gorge, to speak with him," she decided at last. "He can be reached there sometimes, in the encampment by the cottonwood trees that we used so long ago. When you seek him, let your need for Kyra be uppermost, if that's where it fits.

You can't do what you must for your client until you pay attention to it.''

Giving his grandmother's hands a grateful squeeze, David thanked her and exited the hogan. A moment later he was in his pickup, bumping with as much speed as he dared over the rough, barely visible dirt track that led toward the canyon's rim.

Kyra, unknowingly, was close behind him, due to the fact that he'd tarried with his grandmother so long. Afraid she couldn't pinpoint Mary's hogan in the sparse landscape, dotted as it was with other such dwellings, all of them similar, she at last recognized the older woman's crudely nailed-together jewelry stand and turned in beside it.

As she'd been at David's arrival, Mary was standing beside her front door as if she expected her. "Mrs. Many Horses...has David visited you this morning?" she asked, completely forgetting her manners as she jumped out of the Cherokee.

Clearly impervious to gaffes of any sort, Mary nodded. "He was here a few minutes ago," she affirmed. "He went toward the gorge in his truck. It's still possible to follow his dust.''

Chapter Eight

It would be hard on the Cherokee, maybe even damage its shock absorbers and exhaust system. But Kyra didn't give it a second thought. Propelled by an urgent, almost mystical certainty that if she could just catch up with David *now* they could leapfrog past the quandary that was keeping them apart and reach a place of understanding where apologies and recriminations would be irrelevant, she had no other choice.

Thin and rapidly dispersing, the cloud of dust he'd stirred with the wheels of his pickup beckoned. Yet when she reached the spot where he'd parked, a short distance from the canyon rim, the man she sought was nowhere in sight.

Switching off the Cherokee's engine and getting out, she walked over to the pickup and rested her hand on the hood. The surface was still warm enough to suggest that he couldn't be more than a few hundred yards distant. Yet, except for the canyon itself, which carved a deep, undulating fissure in the mostly treeless expanse of high desert and was visible at that distance only as glimpses of pink and

terra-cotta rock that lifted slightly above the surrounding
monotone of grama grass, jimsonweed and bare earth, she
could see in all directions. His tall, denim-clad figure was
missing from the landscape.

Sorry she hadn't worn hiking boots instead of her favorite tasseled loafers, which didn't offer her much traction,
she covered the remaining twenty yards or so of uneven
ground that separated her from the rim. And caught her
breath. Though in a limited sense she'd set eyes on the
Little Colorado's incredible pinks and reds before—catching flashes of them from the highway as she'd passed—she
was overcome by its magnificence.

It's like a cathedral, she thought in amazement, that a
person could enter by climbing down into the nave from
one of its tallest spires. She found it to be more stunning
in its desert nakedness than the Grand Canyon with its lush
environs of ponderosa-pine forest. She drank in its sunset
colors, the silvery sky-reflection that lit its clay-tinged river
and the yellowing fringe of cottonwood trees that drank
from that river's life-giving source. The spontaneous met-
aphor of sanctuary it evoked helped her to see why David
had come to this hauntingly beautiful place four years earlier, seeking comfort.

Did he come here for the same reason today? Or to seek
some answers related to the Naminga case? she wondered,
wishing she'd put the question to his grandmother when
they'd talked briefly a few minutes earlier. Neither under-
taking made sense in a strictly rational context. Yet she
knew with an inner kind of knowing that she'd guessed his
purposes.

Shading her eyes against the sun's brilliance, she scanned
the canyon's crevices and sun-drenched outcroppings, its
flat, coiling riverbed and the dense patches of shade afforded by the cottonwoods. No movement or shape hinted

at a human presence. To all appearances, the Little Colorado was the exclusive domain of snakes and lizards, jackrabbits and butterflies.

Yet David was there. She knew it with the deepest kind of certainty. Unfortunately the canyon was a vast place. Without experience as a tracker, she couldn't hope to guess which route he'd taken. Picking her way along the rim, she searched for a viable way down the cliffs in order to follow him.

Several possibilities presented themselves, all of them hazardous. The most promising, which descended from the point where a stunted, half-dead juniper had thrust its roots into the rim's hard scrabble, seeking moisture, required her to lower herself onto a ledge by clinging with both hands to one of its twisted branches. From there, she might be able to reach a difficult series of finger and toeholds that would take her farther into the canyon's depths.

It had been several years since she'd attempted anything of the sort—five, nearly six to be exact. She was sorely out of practice. As a result, she found herself asking several questions. Was the branch brittle enough to snap? Or would it support her weight? Could she actually make it? There was only one way to find out. Cautiously easing herself down and landing safely on the ledge, she took a deep breath and considered her next move.

On closer inspection, the route she'd chosen seemed even less negotiable than it had first appeared. In fact, the toeholds she'd spotted from above looked as if they might crumble beneath her weight. Unless David could fly like a hawk, sailing with outstretched arms on the canyon's air currents, he must have chosen some other route, she decided, sitting down on an outcropping of rock to survey the situation. But which one? The other choices looked twice as precarious.

Scrambling up to the point where she'd started would be quite a task—one that ran contrary to her intention. It might be best to wait. She had plenty of time. And no compulsion to be anywhere else. If David spotted her, he'd climb up to meet her. Or come looking for her if he returned by a different path and found her Cherokee parked beside his pickup.

Leaning her chin on her hand, she gazed into the chasm that had taken the river eons to create and gave herself up to its exquisite loneliness, the utter timelessness that was the indwelling essence of such a place.

Deep in the gorge, hidden from Kyra's sight by the doorway in time he'd finally managed to slip through, David was seated cross-legged on the earthen floor of an old-style, mud-and-branch hogan, watching with respect and a soul-deep yearning to be led from his difficulties as his great-grandfather created a sand painting from the small piles of colored sand, tinted earth and finely powdered rock an apprentice had placed before him.

Thin gray braids fastened with twists of silver wire framed Henry Many Horses's face as he concentrated on his task. Bare to the waist, he wore just a pair of frayed denim trousers and a braided leather belt. His callused feet were bare, as well. Though his face was lined from the harsh living conditions he'd had to endure for most of his life, he appeared younger than he had at ninety-one, shortly before his death. In fact, he looked much as he had in his late sixties, when David had been eleven or twelve years old.

A *dah nidiilge'e'h*, or deerskin prayer bundle, containing precious bits of earth, twigs and curing plants he'd gathered on long-ago pilgrimages to each of the four sacred Navajo mountains, hung from a cord around his neck. As he worked, he chanted the time-honored words of a curing song beneath his breath.

David had heard the song a hundred times at least, during the various ceremonies he'd attended since he was small. Like his great-grandfather, he knew its words by heart. His keenest attention was claimed by the two groups of stick figures that had begun to people the work of art taking shape beneath Henry Many Horses's earth-stained fingertips.

One group consisted of three men, the other of two men and a woman. In each group, a male figure stood in the middle with outstretched hands, keeping his companions apart. In each, the interloper was white.

Time seemed to stretch to infinity, encompassing both past and future, as David's great-grandfather added a deft touch here, a bit of color there, glancing up at him now and then as if to see if he'd begun to guess at the painting's meaning. It seemed the most natural thing in the world when his grandmother entered the hogan to sit slightly to one side and behind him, a quiet but supportive presence.

Near the canyon's rim, where Kyra had continued to wait for the better part of an hour, the light had shifted. Gradually her thoughts had stilled, leaving her awash in a sensation of pure being. Without anything so formal as calculation, or the slightest need to settle past scores, she longed with all her strength to be reunited with the black-haired, sometimes-difficult-to-understand Navajo defense attorney she still loved. Whatever had happened in the past was gone. Finished. They belonged together. Everything else seemed irrelevant in the canyon's ageless context.

Shifting her focus slightly, she noticed some surprising shadows. They seemed to hint at a path where nothing of the sort had been obvious earlier. Dizzyingly steep, and definitely not for the fainthearted, it appeared to lead in exactly the direction she wanted to go.

Not pausing to give fear a chance to gain the upper hand, or count the damage she was likely to inflict on her person, let alone her clothing, she started down, inching her way to another ledge a dozen feet or so below. To her amazement, more footholds appeared—worn and difficult looking, very much as if they'd been chiseled from the rock wall of the gorge by the Anasazi cliff dwellers of old. An unseen presence seemed to guide her, whispering that whatever bumps and bruises she might sustain would be well worth the cost.

Forty-five minutes and several scrapes later, she was on the canyon floor, splashing across a shallow, relatively tranquil spot in the river to reach the opposite bank. Excitement gripped her as she spotted a thin curl of smoke rising beyond a thicket of cottonwoods. She was sure that smoke hadn't been there before. To my knowledge, no one had lived in this canyon for many years. Maybe David has built a campfire, she thought.

A short walk along the riverbank, which was shadowed now between its sandstone cliffs in the late-afternoon light, brought her to a slightly broader cove. There, among more yellowing cottonwoods, she saw to her surprise that several makeshift Native American dwellings of the type seldom used in the late twentieth century had been lashed together. Nearby, a huge pile of branches had been gathered as if for a fire, perhaps to mark some kind of ceremony.

Should she approach?

There was no sign of David. If there were Native Americans living in the gorge in an attempt to avoid their ancestors' white conquerors and escape the mechanized bustle of late twentieth-century America, they might not thank her for trespassing on their solitude. The Little Colorado was part of their reservation, after all.

She decided to take the chance. Emerging from the cover of the trees, she approached the little settlement politely, diffidently, her downcast eyes begging its residents not to take offense.

The handful of Navajo tribesmen and women she encountered as she ventured closer were dressed in old-style garments. Friendly seeming, almost as if they'd been told to expect her, they greeted her in the Navajo tongue. To her good fortune, she knew a few words of the language, enough to return their salutation, thanks to her upbringing in that part of the world. Yet, beyond that, she couldn't make out much of what they said. They seemed to be speaking an archaic dialect.

In the shadow of one of the hogans, several women were grinding corn in an ancient manner. Approaching them, Kyra spoke David's name, appending a question mark.

To her relief, the youngest of the group spoke English. "Your man is with the shaman," she said in a sweet, husky voice. "They can't be disturbed. You can talk with him later. Come...help us grind the corn for tonight's feast."

Though she'd never participated in such a task before, Kyra willingly accepted the invitation. "What's the occasion?" she asked. "Is it a curing ceremony?"

When the youngest woman translated her words for the others, they were convulsed with shy giggles. Had she made some kind of faux pas? Or inadvertent joke?

Hushing them with an indulgent glance, Kyra's translator smiled at her. "I can only say that the medicine man bade us prepare," she said. "Since your man came, you have been expected."

In the hogan where David was conferring with his great-grandfather, the old man paused in the allegorical chant he was singing about the group of three men in the sand painting and met David's eyes. "Your woman has arrived," he commented.

"You mean...Kyra's *here?*" David blurted, astonished that, without schooling of any sort, she'd managed to walk through a barrier few had traversed—one which frequently defeated him despite the years of tutelage he'd received at Henry Many Horses's knee.

His elderly relatives seemed to take her feat for granted. "Where else does she belong but at your side?" his grandmother asked.

Her logic was irrefutable.

"Nowhere else," he replied, letting the extraordinary rightness of what was happening sink into his bones.

"I have asked the tribe to prepare for your nuptials," his great-grandfather revealed. "I saw long ago in a sand painting that you would marry her here. It was written that if you asked her in the meeting place of your ancestors, she would give you the answer you wish."

Out of respect for his elderly relative, David didn't question the statement. But he couldn't help wondering if things would be as he said, given the stumbling block Kyra had spoken of as they'd lain in their separate beds at the little reservation motel.

As usual his thoughts were transparent to his great-grandfather. "I cannot say what hindrance continues to lie between you, though the answer is represented here," he said, gesturing with one hand toward the sand painting. "It's up to your woman to do that...her responsibility to decide if truth resides in certain claims that have been made to her. Fortunately, as a novice who has slipped through one of the doorways in time that are everywhere about us, she isn't likely to remember it tonight."

Again David remained silent, comforted but far from re-assured.

And again his great-grandfather read his thoughts. "It's true," Henry Many Horses admitted, "that when you return to the everyday world, where your problems reside, your woman may forget the vows you'll speak. The troubles that have separated you so long may regain their force. Nevertheless, a bond will have been forged. If you can retain your inner peace, though you must struggle to do it and let her make whatever discoveries she needs to make, ultimately it will have the power to bring you together."

After helping with the corn—a task that seemed to instill repose and a sense of fatalism in her—Kyra watched the women fry what she thought of as johnnycakes on a griddle over a small open fire. Rabbit meat and peach crisp with piñon nuts were set to bake among the ashes. For some reason the woman who'd spoken English to her took a small amount of the freshly ground corn meal and added water, cooking it into a mush that would feed one or two people, at best.

No one challenged Kyra when, with nothing further to do and only a tenuous attachment to the group, she got to her feet and wandered off to explore the encampment. With the bemused gaze of an outsider, she watched three small children play a game with sticks and bones in the dust and a man stake some ponies out to graze. Those ponies must have been brought in through the gorge's mouth, many miles distant, she thought. There's no way they could have clambered down its steep rock walls.

Another man sat cross-legged outside one of the hogans, which was set apart. Though he appeared to be half-asleep, dreaming in the sun, something about the way his body was arranged barred the entrance. It must be the medicine man's hogan, she realized. If so, David's inside, as the woman said.

Though the intensity of her longing to see the dark-haired man she'd taken such risks to follow had continued to expand and grow, she found herself uncharacteristically willing to wait the required number of hours until he emerged.

They'll tell him I'm here. He'll come and find me. When we meet, there'll be no barriers, she thought, turning away and strolling a little farther along the riverbank as the reflected hues of the setting sun kindled the copper-colored water and tinged the piled-up clouds that were massing overhead.

That there'd *been* an obstacle, she had little doubt. The sense of urgency that had preceded her deepening peace bore ample witness to it. Yet, try though she would, she couldn't recall its nature. It can't have been so very important, she concluded, sitting down on a fallen log and letting what was left of the day settle about her. The possibility that her father might be out of his mind with worry over her unexplained absence for the second night in a row didn't even enter her head.

Dusk had siphoned away most of the light, and the sucked-to-transparency cough drop of the moon was clearly visible above the canyon rim by the time David approached her on silent feet. How slender and delicate she looks, this woman I love, he marveled as, undetected, he studied her meditative pose. He wanted to protect her with all his strength. Yet he knew she could be as persistent as a Navajo pony in a snowstorm, well able to care for herself.

He was amazed that after her categorical rejection of him, she'd climbed down into the gorge unaided to renew their contact. What a resourceful seeker she is, he thought, to have followed me here through the kind of doorway only a deep communion with spirit can open. And what an intuitive being, to know where to look. He surmised that although she'd probably never called it into play before, she had a gift for transcending the limits of everyday existence that might someday surpass the one he'd worked so hard to cultivate.

If she would have him, what a team they'd make! Fighting injustice and saving innocents like Paul Naminga from a misguided criminal justice system in their working mode, they'd love each other to sleep at night in their private life and make beautiful babies together. He'd been nothing short of a fool, failing to recognize the priceless gift she'd been offering him when he'd run from her five years earlier.

He only hoped he hadn't recognized its value too late.

Seldom mistaken about such things, his great-grandfather had speculated that she wouldn't carry her burden of accusation into the gorge. If he asked her to marry him here, Henry Many Horses had told him, he'd get the response he wished. Unfortunately he'd warned in the same breath that when they resumed their lives in the present-day world, she might forget their promises, renew her grudge against him.

If the bond they forged was strong enough, maybe their love would survive the transfer. In a voice that conveyed the deep longing and anticipation he felt, he spoke her name aloud, just the single word.

David had come for her. Snatched from her reverie by a rush of happiness so strong it pierced her to the quick, Kyra leaped to her feet. Seconds later she was in his arms, woven more tightly to his being than fingers can interlace.

Incredibly they'd come home in each other. They were free of impediments and recriminations in that stunning place. Like an avalanche that was all consuming, yet incredibly tender, his mouth took possession of hers. With all her heart, she yielded it, ready to lie down with him among the fallen leaves and give him everything she possessed.

It was what he wanted, too. But he couldn't let her give it to him yet. Their years apart and the influence of his great-grandfather's wisdom had forced him to take the larger scheme of things into consideration. He wanted more from Kyra than a passionate tumble, a release from tension and longing that came without promises. In addition to his love and protection, he wanted to offer her honor and respect.

In the simplest of terms, he wanted her to be his wife. To give her children. Both passion and dailiness. The chance to grow old as her closest companion, the husband she loved. "Marry me," he begged. "You're the only woman who's ever laid claim to my heart."

It was what she'd secretly wanted from the moment she'd set eyes on him, that long-ago summer when she'd come home from her second year of law school to find him working on her father's staff. As easily as laughing with a friend or quaffing a beer after work, lithe, raven-haired, appealingly exotic David Yazzie had commandeered her separateness.

"The feast they're preparing is in our honor," he prodded when joy held her speechless. "Say yes. I love you so much."

In her dream—for surely she was still sleeping on her rock in the sun, a little below the canyon rim—the issue of his accepting a bribe for walking out on her didn't exist.

"Yes, David," she whispered. "Oh, yes. I love you, too. There's nothing on earth I want as much."

His answer was another kiss, so deep and all consuming that the two of them could drown in it.

They were wearing faded jeans, the most casual of clothing. But no one seemed to mind as they returned to the encampment with their arms about each other—two people who, in their hearts, had become one though they hadn't consummated their union yet.

Their faces glowing with approval, the men and women of the gorge accepted them as they were. Her hand in David's, belonging there by right, Kyra bowed her head as heavy ceremonial necklaces of turquoise and silver were placed about their necks.

"It's almost time," the young English-speaking tribeswoman who'd translated for Kyra earlier alerted them with a smile. "You should take your places."

As she spoke, several of the men lit torches and touched them to the brushpile, causing it to catch and blaze up in a giant *whoosh* of flames. Sparks scattered like fireflies on the breeze as the bone-dry brush crackled and hissed. A tapestry of light and darkness washed over strong-boned faces, giving the dreamlike scene an even more surreal aspect.

To Kyra's surprise, David's grandmother emerged from the hogan where he'd conferred with the shaman and came, smiling, to stand next to them. Perhaps it was the firelight, with its capacity for illusion. But to Kyra she appeared younger—less marked by her journey through life than she'd seemed during their brief conversation before she'd driven off toward the canyon, following David's dust.

In what must surely be a dream, though her heightened senses argued otherwise, Kyra didn't find Mary Many Horses's presence in the canyon all that astonishing. Yet she was bowled over by the knowledge and discernment that radiated from the older woman's face with the veils of everyday vision swept aside.

There wasn't time to remark on her observation. Or question it. Following Mary from the hogan was a hawk-faced older man in a black velvet shirt and denims who wore a deerhide pouch on a thong around his neck and what appeared to be a priceless collection of turquoise jewelry about his person. His dark eyes glowed with wisdom, compassion and insight.

He was the shaman, of course. And more. Though they'd never met, Kyra knew him also to be David's great-grandfather, the tribal elder and medicine man he'd always respected so much.

"I thought your great-grandfather died several years ago," she whispered, suddenly a little frightened by what was taking place. "Tell me this is real...that I'm not just dreaming it."

Tugging her closer still, David caused her to rest a hand against his chest for support. "Can you feel my breath feathering your cheek?" he asked with deep affection, his mouth all but grazing it. "Sense the drumbeat of my love for you wherever our bodies touch?"

She could. And did. Oh, she did....

Allowing herself to trust, and glory in the luck and happiness that had found her, she lowered her head with respect as his great-grandfather approached, then raised it when he began to speak. Her *yes* was as steady as the ground on which they stood when the old man asked them each in turn if they'd agreed to make a life together.

Chapter Nine

The ceremony in which Henry Many Horses joined Kyra and David Yazzie by firelight beneath a ribbon of desert sky thickly encrusted with stars was the essence of simplicity, yet so profound it easily annihilated their separateness. At its core were plainspoken vows to love and trust, forsaking any wish for others. To open their hearts if the Great Spirit gave them children. Ultimately to bring honor to the tribe and to all people with their every married word and gesture.

"Will you do these things?" David's great-grandfather asked, giving him an expectant, deeply serious look.

"I will do them," the man Kyra loved promised in a voice that reverberated with emotion. As he spoke, he laced his fingers so tightly with hers that in the tender little interstices between them, their pulses throbbed to a single drumbeat.

The old man turned to Kyra, his ebony eyes like glowing coals as they gave back the fire's incandescence. "What do you say, woman of his choosing?'' he demanded, fixing her with his hawklike gaze. ''Will you do them, as well?''

In that setting, where past and present formed a single thread and the heart was its only compass, Kyra could think of no impediment. She only knew that she would love the blue-eyed, part-Navajo attorney who had stolen her heart until she drew her last breath. With every particle of her being, she longed to melt into him, join with him so completely that they could never be separated.

''I will do them,'' she whispered.

She's mine, David thought, the unanticipated wonder of what was happening between them piercing him to the quick. My wife. The companion of my soul. In the deepest sense, an integral part of myself.

It took every bit of moderation he possessed not to gather her into his arms on the spot—claim her with the kind of passionate kiss that, in the vast ocean of Hispanic and Anglo-Saxon culture that surrounded the last remaining native inhabitants of the American Southwest, might be forthcoming at such a moment.

With his Navajo soul, he realized that any such action would offend his relatives and their wedding guests, not to mention compromise the moment's sacredness. Besides, the ceremony wasn't over. A final seal on their union remained to be set.

At a beckoning glance from her elderly father, the shaman, Mary Many Horses stepped forward, her face wreathed in smiles of approbation, to offer them a round, flat basket woven of sumac fiber that had been dyed to produce a red, gray and ivory twelve-pointed design. The basket contained a little mound of the cornmeal mush the young woman who'd spoken English to her had cooked with such care that afternoon.

What were they supposed to do with it? No initiate in

Navajo ceremonies, Kyra didn't have a clue. Glancing from one expectant, firelit face to another, she tried to guess what was expected of them.

Steeped in the customs of his native tribe since childhood, despite the other ethnic strains that made up his heritage, David came to her rescue. Taking a pinch of the mush between his fingertips, he held it out for her to eat.

The gesture was clearly a sacramental one. Like a woman in a dream, yet so wholly present in the moment that every nerve ending in her body was firing with anticipation, she allowed him to put the morsel of mush in her mouth.

Intimate, holy, the sensation of his fingers parting her lips, so that they were in contact with her tongue as she tasted the mush's naturally sweet graininess, was for her a loving, almost erotic precursor of what they'd do together. Its foreshadowing of their communion-to-be sent a pang of need for deeper, more intimate contact winging to her deepest places, almost as if he had stroked her breasts.

Her instinctive grasp of the gesture's significance caused David's eyes to glitter with corresponding arousal as she returned the favor. Without having to be told, he guessed in that moment how it would be with them—foresaw their breathless disrobing and fierce yet reverent taking, the mystical merging in coitus of their souls, their separateness. Reaching for the heavens, they'd burn like the comets the early seers and medicine men among his people had regarded as wondrous portents.

To celebrate their union, a chant broke out among the women. The men danced, sending up a cloud of dust with the age-old pattern of their footsteps. Sparks from the fire blew on the breeze as drummers kept time, each of their drums speaking with its own percussive voice.

At last the old shaman pronounced the simple but profound ceremony complete.

"In beauty it is finished. Go now...with beauty behind you, beauty in front of you," he said, a look of benevolence softening his creased face. "It's time to begin your married life together."

Their hands clasped, their shoulders lightly touched in blessing and congratulation by a small group of well-wishers that included David's approving great-grandfather and his smiling grandmother, they were free to go. Joined to David, with one of his strong arms securely wound about her waist and her head leaning against his shoulder, Kyra allowed him to lead her gently away from the encampment and its bonfire, toward the riverbank.

In a way she found it difficult to believe any of the things she was experiencing were actually taking place. Maybe I'm really dozing on a rock in the sun, she thought. Or in my Cherokee, parked above the canyon rim, just dreaming this.

In contradiction to that possibility, her eyes were wide open. She could smell the fire's piñon-juniper perfume rising in the night sky and hear its distant crackling. Without question she could feel David's strong hands gripping her. The quiet lapping of the river kept audible rhythm with her breath.

Incredibly, David Yazzie, with his keen intellect and heart-stopping physique, his passionate Native-American complexity, had vowed to cherish her, forsaking all others. He was her husband now, after so much longing. When they came together in the fullness of their conjugal embrace, their attainment would fill the universe.

Never had she felt so lucky, so utterly and completely blessed. Having lived without the only man she wanted for five star-crossed, empty years, she was overcome that life could be so generous. She dismissed a fleeting notion that all was not yet settled between them as casually as she might untangle a willow branch that had caught in her hair, or brush aside an annoying insect.

For his part, David wanted to pinch himself. After rejecting him without agreeing to fully share her reasons for doing so, Kyra had reversed herself. She'd promised to love him and care for him for the rest of his days. Without protest she was letting him lead her toward the marriage hogan. Next to the fire he would build beneath its traditional smoke hole, she'd let him take her with a litany of cries and whispers.

Whatever else he did, he vowed, he'd make it last. They'd wasted too much time already to let precious moments slip like water through the Little Colorado into the past. Instead of haste and the quick assuagement of longing, he wanted a slow, impassioned buildup to the cadence of a breaking thunderstorm—one that promised a healing downpour in its wake.

I've probably loved her since the day she first walked into Big Jim Frakes's office, a green kid still in law school hired to help out for the summer, he thought.

She'd been so intelligent and beautifully made, with the innocence she couldn't hide shining forth from her big, green eyes. He couldn't deny her slim hips and rounded bosom had caught his eye, as well. Like a powerful aphrodisiac, her instantaneous attraction to him had ignited him.

Her shy, somewhat erudite observation that, given the fact he was homozygous recessive for eye color, he must have Anglo genes on both sides of his family tree, had amused and deepened his interest in her. *She knows a lot about a lot of things,* he'd realized. *And she likes half-*

breeds. From the look on her face, she probably thinks I'm a little dangerous, he'd thought back then.

Now she was everything to him. Their ethnic differences were mere titillation, erotic icing on the cake. Yet a part of him still gloried in them. Imagining how the scene might unfold from above as he fused his onyx and copper hues to her ivory, Scandinavian-blond loveliness in the blaze of their first lovemaking had him hard to bursting.

They'd reached a spot where the river ran close to the canyon's north wall and, without ceremony, he scooped her up to carry her across the little cove of cold, shallow water that separated them from the cottonwoods where their marriage hogan waited.

By now the bonfire at the encampment where they'd pledged their troth was a distant flicker of reddish hues. Only the moon held sway, mimicked by the match he struck to light their progress into the small, mud-and-branch hovel to which his great-grandfather had directed them.

Glancing about her, Kyra saw little more than some hand-loomed blankets piled on an earthen floor, a fire pit containing a small pile of branches, and a smoke hole in the roof which afforded a temporary glimpse of stars. We'll sleep like rocks, wrapped in those blankets, after we've used up every dram of energy we possess making love to each other, she predicted to herself.

"David?" she asked, unable to keep herself from prodding him.

"I'll light the fire for us," he answered in a husky voice, pulling off his scuffed, tooled-leather cowboy boots. "Once it's burning, we can take off our things. I don't want the shadows to swallow up any of our shivers. Or obscure a single goose bump."

As he bent to kindle the sticks and small branches that had been laid for them, Kyra remembered how on several occasions, in the shabby rented trailer where he'd lived when he was courting her five years earlier, they'd come achingly close to making love. Now there'd be nothing to hold them back. They'd reach for the stars. David would fill her deepest places, explode inside her like a supernova as they rode each other to paradise.

Catching her by surprise, the realization that he might not have brought protection with him into the gorge excited her still further. If he did bring it, I don't want him to use it, she thought with amorous perversity. I want to be the seedbed of his longing, his plow's willing furrow.

Just the thought of it had her wet and trembling.

By now the fire had caught and begun to burn, sending a spicy curl of smoke upward toward the roof's small opening. Straightening from his task, David caught hold of her hands and stroked their palms with his fingertips. The light but suggestive touch only caused her craving to deepen.

"Kyra...sweetheart...you'll never know how often I've lain awake in my bed at the ranch or in my motor-home bunk, while I was defending a client on the road, unable to stop thinking about you," he confessed, removing his ceremonial necklace and setting it aside. "I can't begin to count the times I've imagined us beneath Havasu Falls, with your swimsuit top swirling away on the current as I caressed your breasts. Let's take off our things so we can look our fill."

Of all the encounters that had gone into the making of their unconsummated love affair five years earlier, he'd chosen *that* one to mention—the very one she'd been dreaming about when her father had awakened her with his call and begged her to return to Flagstaff. Though her memory-erasing trip into the gorge had temporarily obscured most recent events from her head along with any recollection of what she'd considered David's treachery, she was able to recall the bare bones of that telephone conversation. On the other hand, the army surplus tent she and David had used to camp in Havasu Canyon and their hairbreadth retreat from consummation beneath its famous cascade, seemed as fresh as yesterday.

Like a flash of heat lightning, a connection arced between the longing that had almost overcome them beneath the falls and another, seemingly more recent occasion when she'd denied herself a wordlessly offered chance to make love to him.

She couldn't pinpoint the time or place where it had happened. All she knew was that David had been standing unclothed beside what might have been a swimming pool. And she'd lingered in the water, watching the slow-motion spectacle that ensued as he put on a robe. Moments later, when she'd followed in her own nakedness, he'd done his share of looking as well.

If her blurry memory served, he'd kept his hands to himself.

"So long as touching's allowed," she agreed, removing her necklace, also, and pulling her sweater over her head, followed by her T-shirt.

Small but lush, her breasts swung free. Uncertain how much she could recall in their current setting, David guessed at once what had prompted her edict. "If you think I'll leave you untouched on our wedding night, White Shell Woman, you're certifiable," he shot back, his arousal burgeoning.

Fumbling with the tarnished, handmade silver buttons of his black buckskin shirt, David removed it to reveal the rippling muscles of his chest and arms. Courtesy of the Anglo and Hispanic blood he could claim on both sides of his family, his chest was covered by a modest inverted triangle of coal black hair that tapered against his coppery skin into a narrow, downward-pointing seam.

As Kyra knew, one-hundred-percent Native Americans usually had smooth bodies. She'd always regarded David's dark, masculine furring as a symbol of the fortuitous ethnic stew that had made him the special man he was.

In response to a questioning look from him, she unsnapped the waistband of her jeans and tugged down her zipper. Seconds later she was stepping out of them. Her bikini panties followed, to be added to the little heap of clothing at her feet. With a heart full of love, she offered him her nakedness.

Wild to have her, to connect with her so deeply that if trouble came, it wouldn't be able to tear them apart, David was out of his jeans and shorts in seconds, offering his lean hips and thighs, his beautifully hung maleness in return.

Since coming back to Flagstaff, Kyra had glimpsed him like that just once—on the dreamlike occasion by the pool that she couldn't quite recall. Vague or not, the recollection had been more than sufficient to fuel her longing. The chance to look her fill at his tawny physique, with its quickened male attributes and exquisitely developed muscular contours, made her go weak-kneed with desire.

"David," she breathed, the single word both a plea and an invitation.

"We'll have each other, never fear," he promised, matching palms with her so that their fingertips were touching.

If he took her now, with no slow, sweet initiation, he'd probably go off like a rocket. And she might not be ready to accompany his ascent. Of course, he could satisfy her afterward. Or attempt to take her with him in a second go-round.

But he didn't want it to be that way on their wedding

night. Instead, he wanted their first release to be both mutual and simultaneous—a slow, sweet buildup to the kind of helplessness no earthly being could resist, as achingly and wondrously complete as he could make it.

The surest way to guarantee that outcome would be to make love to her in the ancient way his great-grandfather had once described as the most erotic, yet spiritual connection a man and woman could make.

As a way of priming them both, he knelt before her on their wedding blankets to cup her breasts. Kyra gasped with pleasure as he captured one erect, rosy nipple with his mouth and sucked at it, gently flipping it back and forth with his tongue. Simultaneously, he massaged her other bud into tight submission. The intimate caresses telegraphed urgent messages of need to her deepest places.

"David. *Oh, David. I want you so,*" she told him in smothered supplication, tangling her fingers in his straight, dark hair as his kisses dipped to her navel. "Please...make love to me."

It was what he wanted, too—so much that he'd burn to ashes if they deferred another second. Yet suddenly he was remembering the lapse she'd speculated about earlier. He'd been convinced that when they met again it would be in Judge Beamish's courtroom, consequently the single prophylactic he'd taken—just in case—to the small reservation motel where they'd spent the previous night was no longer available to them. The morning after their falling-out, he'd taken it from the pocket of his jeans and tossed it into one of the motel room's beat-up plastic wastebaskets. He didn't have any form of protection to offer her.

Though it was their wedding night, he couldn't join her in consummation. His great-grandfather had warned him that once they were out of the gorge and back in their everyday lives, Kyra might not remember anything of their wedding vows. Yet she might very well recall the unnamed barrier she'd refused to discuss with him. To saddle her with his child under those circumstances was unthinkable.

"I can't do it, babe," he confessed with an aching heart. "I never dreamed you'd follow me here. Or that you'd be willing to become my wife. I didn't bring protection."

To his surprise and amazement, she seemed already to have guessed the situation. And discounted it with loving recklessness.

"I had a strong feeling that was probably the case," she admitted. "And I'm willing to take the risk. If it comes about as a result of what we do tonight, having your baby would bring me the greatest happiness."

With a little groan of love and gratitude, he sat cross-legged on the blankets that had been laid for them and held out his arms.

"Cover me, then...sit on my lap and take me inside you," he entreated. "Cradle me with your knees and hold me close."

It wasn't the kind of position she'd expected him to propose. He'd never so much as hinted that he liked to make love that way. Still, wet with arousal in the place where she wanted him most and quivering with anticipation, she trusted him enough to follow his suggestion.

A little cry of satisfaction escaped her as, for the first time in their uneven history, he was sheathed in her depths. I have all of him now, she exulted—absolutely everything he has to give. We're connected as intimately as the cells of a single body. If we tried, we could think each other's thoughts. Feel each other's deepest yearnings.

To her surprise, though David was throbbing with longing inside her, he didn't move. The expression on his face, which appeared half-blind and thoroughly Navajo in the shifting light, told her he was fighting for mastery of himself.

She didn't want their lovemaking to be over in seconds, either, despite an almost overpowering need to feel him thrusting against her most sensitive places. I'll follow his lead, she decided, wondering even as she made it if she could keep that kind of bargain for long.

For what seemed forever, but in reality was only a minute or so, they continued in the same way, allowing themselves just the most limited and tantalizing of movements.

By some incomprehensible logic, the restraint they were practicing seemed to ignite them more profoundly than the most impassioned writhing could have done. Yet, by its very nature, the bounds they had placed on themselves couldn't endure for long. With a sheer precipitousness that dazzled her, Kyra found herself losing control. Her vow to be led, not lead, crumbling, she tightened her strong interior muscles, clasping David in the most intimate possible embrace.

Ecstasy and an expression of soul-deep rapture washed over his aquiline features as he thrust deeper to accommodate her, then reverted to the subtle, slowly elaborating fullness that had primed the pump of her desire to such fierce intensity. Ignited by the fullness of him and his single, answering thrust, a hot, diffuse glow began to spread through her body.

"Ah, but I love you," David confessed, his face so close to hers that neither of them could see the other's features clearly as he kissed her mouth.

As I love you, she responded silently, knowing he'd catch her answer as easily as if she'd spoken aloud.

By mutual consent, they continued in that vein for several more minutes, with David thrusting each time the ripples of feeling became too much for them. Each time, Kyra answered by clasping him tightly and dragging him deeper still.

Little by little, their sense of inevitability grew more intense. Their control slipped, causing their movements to take on a greater urgency.

For the first time in Kyra's twenty-seven years, her womanhood was abundantly in flower, her instincts as old as humankind and deep as the universe.

He's the first man for me, she reflected wildly. As I'm his first woman. It's as if Brad—and David's previous lovers—didn't exist.

With the thought, her thighs tensed and her body bent like a bowstring, reaching for consummation. Eager to continue at the lip of desire, she tried to stop herself. But it was too late.

Like one leap of fire touching off another, her shudders ignited his, consuming them both. Gooseflesh passed like a storm from skin to skin, as their cries of rapture lifted through the hogan roof with the piñon smoke to echo from the canyon walls.

Little by little they quieted. Kyra remained on David's lap, with her knees cradling him. Beading on their skin, their sweat mingled with the blunt, exhausted kisses they exchanged. Nothing of the passion and release that had rocked them was hidden. The warmth of quiescence flooded them as they continued to sit face-to-face.

"In beauty it is finished," David said at last when he could speak, echoing his great-grandfather's words with reverence as he tenderly framed her face.

It was the traditional seal set on every Navajo ceremony, including their marriage vows—a paean to radiance, mystery and appropriateness, the fitting participation of humans in what was in essence a godlike activity.

"In beauty...and so much love," she answered.

"All my love is yours," he echoed.

Easing her from his lap, David invited her to lie beside him and pulled one of the blankets over them. But they weren't finished yet. Talking, kissing and caressing each other with sweet possessiveness between rounds, they made love twice more that night—somewhat more traditionally, to be sure, but with the bliss of their first encounter to guide them and relight the Roman candle of their longing. It wasn't until 2 a.m. by David's watch that they finally called it a night and twined together in sleep on the hard, blanket-covered ground.

Her body cramped and her left cheek aching from being pillowed against the window frame on the driver's side, Kyra awoke six hours later, behind the wheel of her Cherokee. She was alone. David's truck, which had been parked next to her vehicle when she'd halted there the previous afternoon, was nowhere in sight.

Meanwhile, a passionate, almost mythic dream she seemed to have had just before awakening was fleeing her memory in tantalizing wisps—too swiftly for her to fix many of its details in her consciousness. In it, she and David had been lovers. She guessed that much. Still, the exact nature of the relationship her deeper self had spun for them was difficult to grasp. Instinct whispered that there'd been some kind of ceremony....

In the real world, where happy outcomes were sadly in short supply, she recalled scrambling down the beginnings of a trail into the gorge and giving up at a sheer drop-off to sit on a rock and think things over. She must have decided there was no way she could make it to the bottom and come back up again to wait for him. Why couldn't she clearly remember it?

Bitterness took root at the realization that he must have returned by whatever secret trail he knew, found her asleep and left her there with a shrug of his shoulders—simply gotten into his truck and driven away. Her renewed sense of abandonment was like cholla thorns pricking her flesh. *He doesn't care about me. Or how I feel. I was just handy the night before last, when he came on to me at that shabby little motel,* she thought. *I'll be damned if I'll put myself in a vulnerable position with him again.*

Rubbing the remnants of sleep from her eyes and smoothing her hair into some semblance of order, she started the Cherokee's engine. Fury and humiliation compelled her to drive a little too fast over the dirt track that led to Mary Many Horses's hogan before joining the highway. As a result her tires skidded on the soft earth when she slammed on the brakes at the sight of David's truck.

It was parked just beyond his grandmother's hogan. Stripped to the waist, David himself was chopping wood. As if he'd never noticed her Cherokee parked next to his pickup and abandoned her to his own devices, he put down his ax and raised a hand in greeting. To her surprise, there was an inquiring, painfully tentative look on his face.

I'd be crazy even to get out and talk to him, she thought, even as she reached for the door handle.

She doesn't remember, he realized, his heart sinking to his boots. *All the old demons are back to haunt us.*

"Looking for me?" he asked.

By now, her painful memories of the way he'd left her five years earlier were firmly back in place.

She shook her head. "I just wanted to thank Mary for letting me spend the night on her property," she said stiffly. "I guess I needn't tell you I was here. You must have seen me, asleep in the Cherokee, when you came for your truck."

A small silence ensued, during which they gazed at each other from the opposite sides of a very high fence. *I should* have roused her, he thought. God knows I wanted to. But Great-Grandfather had said...

"As a matter of fact, I did," he admitted at last. "You were sleeping so soundly I hated to wake you. What were you doing there, anyway?"

About to confess the reason for her U-turn from Gray Mountain Trading Post to the gorge and his grandmother's hogan, Kyra decided to hold her tongue. Though her heart was crying out, her scruples over the money she believed he had taken from her father to abandon her had returned. She didn't want David to know how much she cared for him.

"What does it matter?" she answered. "Maybe I just needed a place to sit and think about where I'm headed next in life. The canyon rim was as good as any."

His beautiful eyes were unreadable. "Did you come to any conclusions?" he asked.

She nodded. "There's nothing in Flagstaff for me anymore. I'll probably head back to Kansas City for a while...maybe take some postgraduate classes and teach at a law school somewhere."

Too eloquent by half, the expression on his face might have betrayed the depth of his feelings for her. He didn't let it. Turning away to finish chopping the wood his grandmother needed and get himself under control, David didn't gaze after her as she walked to Mary's hogan and took up a polite, waiting posture outside its entrance.

Mary emerged almost immediately, as if she'd been expecting her. To Kyra's surprise, the older woman didn't pose any awkward questions about her continued presence on Navajo grazing lands.

"Please...come in," she invited, her dark eyes quickly searching those of her visitor before shuttering any hint of the question they'd contained. "As you probably know, David's here. Why don't you join us for breakfast?"

Mumbling something about not wanting to impose, Kyra declined, adding her thanks for Mary's unsolicited hospitality.

"I hadn't planned to spend the night," she admitted. "I wanted to talk to David, that's all. As it turned out, I wasn't able to catch up with him yesterday afternoon. I fell asleep in the Cherokee, waiting. We, er, managed to exchange a few words just now."

Mary appeared to take her refusal for mere politeness. "You must be hungry," she reiterated. "Stay and eat."

Giving in, Kyra bent to follow her hostess through the hogan's low doorway. The mingled scents of corn bread, fried apples and coffee emanated from the battered pots that were positioned over her cooking fire. She'd been seated for just a moment when David joined them.

To Kyra, his quiet greeting, "I'm glad you could stay," resonated curiously like an invitation to remember some shared secret.

If there *was* such a secret, she couldn't imagine what it involved. Overwhelmed by feelings of embarrassment during the meal that followed, particularly when David's eyes met hers, she was reticent, all but silent, joining in the conversation with any verve only when he and Mary referred to the Naminga case.

Citing a need to return to Flagstaff, as her father was bound to be worried about her, she announced her departure as soon as the meal was finished. To her chagrin, David insisted on walking her to her vehicle.

If he isn't going to tell me the truth about what he did five years ago, I don't want to get into another postmortem with him, she thought, her heart aching as she glanced up at his handsome face before sliding behind the wheel. Having to discuss the situation further would only make matters worse.

"Goodbye, then," she said as noncommittally as she could, inserting her key in the ignition.

She'd left the window down on the driver's side and, evocative as only he could be, he rested a hand on her shoulder.

"When am I going to see you again?" he asked.

At the physical contact, a rush of memory evoked by the dream she'd had just before awakening welled up so vividly it gave her a little shudder of déjà vu.

Common sense insisted she discount it. "I'm not sure," she answered. "In a courtroom, I suppose. Though we managed to corroborate Paul's story about the boys who'd been sniffing glue, we haven't proven his innocence. You might want to take another look at Ben Monongye's enemies. But if you can't find anything new that exonerates Paul, I'll have to help my dad prosecute."

It was her final word on the subject, David realized. He watched her drive away with an empty feeling in his gut. Were the vows they'd spoken and the rapture they'd shared simply to evanesce like a puff of smoke? Or could they cross the fragile bridge of belief and trust to a life in the present moment?

With effort he remembered his great-grandfather's counsel. According to Henry Many Horses, hidden barriers raised by another—the central male figure in the group of two men and one woman that had comprised part of the sand painting—remained to separate them. To win Kyra back and keep her for a lifetime, he'd have to be patient. According to his great-grandfather, if her love matched his, she'd overcome the barrier herself and remember what had taken place, come back to him. Instead of existing as a memory lost in time, their marriage would unfold in the present moment.

And if she can't? he wondered, clenching his fists in frustration as he watched her dust disperse. Will I be condemned to walk through life alone, missing the biggest piece of my heart?

Chapter Ten

Kyra's father was pacing the front hall and growling something she couldn't catch into his cellular phone when she walked in the door. At 9:30 a.m., he should have been at his desk in the courthouse. Here we go, she thought, bracing herself.

A burly man roughly six feet in height, with thinning hair and slightly stooped shoulders, Big Jim Frakes tended toward affability, a laid-back demeanor and the unpretentious good manners of a true Western gentleman. At the moment, however, he looked irritable enough to whip his string tie loose from its turquoise-studded slide and wrap it around her neck.

"So there you are!" he exploded, brusquely ending his call. "Missing two days and then waltzing in as if you hadn't caused anyone a speck of worry. What the hell was I supposed to think?"

Kyra's jaw jutted slightly in a mannerism she'd learned from him. "That I'm a grown woman who can take care of herself," she answered. "I suppose that's too much to expect."

As she spoke, a disconcerting thought flitted through her head. "You didn't call Red Miner...ask him to have his deputies keep their eyes peeled for me, I hope," she added.

The half-guilty look on his face told her the guess was right on target.

"Dad!" she cried with an exasperated shake of her head. "How could you? I'm so embarrassed!" Pausing, she gentled her tone a little. "I *left* you a note."

"I got it." The admission was a grudging one. "As I recall," he said, "it mentioned something about being back 'tonight or tomorrow.' That was Wednesday. This is Friday. For all I knew, you could have been in an accident. Lying dead somewhere. Now that you've turned up in one piece, I can't help but think you were consorting with..."

Visibly stopping himself, he finished lamely, "The opposition in the Naminga case."

He'd been on the verge of saying "that half-breed" or something similar. And Kyra knew it. About to defend David from the unuttered slur, she held her tongue. Though she ached for his touch with a piercing sense of loss, he didn't deserve her loyalty or affection.

Big Jim took her lack of a response for an admission of guilt. His frown deepened. "Haven't you learned anything yet, gal?" he asked. "You of all people should know that David Yazzie is out for whatever he can get. He'd be contented as a rattlesnake in a woodpile to win your sympathy and help in freeing his client...not to mention get himself a taste of what he missed five years ago."

Kyra's cheeks reddened. Overwhelmed by a sense of loyalty to David unlike any she'd experienced, despite the unfeeling way she believed he'd treated her, she couldn't bring herself to second her father's condemnation.

"You're right about one thing," she conceded, causing him to wince. "I *was* with David. But it wasn't what you think. We drove onto the rez in hopes of finding the boys Paul Naminga claimed were sniffing glue the afternoon of the dance festival. I thought that if they existed and David managed to interview them, we'd want to know everything they said…not just what he chose to give us on discovery."

Annoyed as he was, Big Jim was definitely interested. "So…did you find them?" he asked.

She nodded. "Though it'll probably get them into big trouble with their parents, they confirmed Paul's story. The time frame's going to be awfully tight…" She sketched it out for him. "But I doubt if, by itself, their testimony will get Paul off the hook. He'd still have had enough time to put on his costume, kill Ben Monongye and arrive onstage five minutes late."

To her relief her father appeared somewhat mollified. "Though we don't have an eyewitness to the crime, we've got plenty of circumstantial evidence," he agreed, abandoning the issue of David for the moment. "The fight, the blood on Paul's outfit, the girl who saw someone dressed in a *Koyemsi* costume identical to his enter Ben's trailer…"

Still face-to-face in the entry hall, they stood there looking at each other for a moment.

"I don't suppose I have any right to ask," Big Jim added with characteristic stubbornness. "But I'd like to know where you spent the last two nights."

The pain of hoping David would admit to taking her father's bribe and apologize, which had ended in disappointment, pricked her heart. Out of pride, she kept her feelings under wraps.

"You're right…it *is* none of your business, Dad," she said evenly. "I'll tell you because I choose to do so, in order to set your mind at rest. Though I spent Wednesday night in a motel on the reservation with David, we slept in separate beds. Nothing happened. Thursday night I was alone, thinking things through. I slept in the Cherokee, near the Little Colorado Gorge.''

Big Jim knew as well as anyone that David's grandmother lived near the gorge. But he didn't stoop to pointing that out. "You come to any conclusions?" he asked instead, clearly bracing himself.

Kyra decided to be frank, though she was well aware his worries were based on narrow-mindedness.

"I won't deny I'm still attracted to David," she confessed. "You know that, anyway. But I realize we could never make a go of it. That's not because he's part Navajo…far from it. It's one of the things I like about him. I just can't let myself trust him after the way he behaved five years ago…unless he admits without prompting to taking the money you offered him. And apologizes. That didn't happen. After our most recent conversation about the past, I don't expect it to.''

For some reason, instead of satisfaction, Big Jim's weathered face wore a guilty, embarrassed look. "Ah, baby," he muttered with partially downcast eyes. "I'm sorry about the pain all this has caused. I shouldn't ask so many damn fool questions.''

Though she continued to chafe at his prejudice, Kyra's heart went out to him. "It's okay, Dad," she comforted. "I know that from your perspective, you've always thought of my best interests.''

Under Arizona law, a defendant received a speedy trial unless his or her attorney asked for more time and the judge granted it. To everyone's surprise, on Monday David petitioned Hank Beamish for a continuance in order to dig up some additional witnesses. And got his wish. The trial was reset to a date that would push it past Kyra's intended stay in Flagstaff. During the remaining weeks of her visit, she'd be able to help her father refine his case and plan for its presentation to the jury. But she wouldn't be there in person to help him argue it.

Predictably, Big Jim was furious. "David Yazzie did this for the sole purpose of depriving me of your assistance on my last big case," he complained to Kyra as they returned to his office from Judge Beamish's chambers. "He's hoping it'll make me nervous, having to go up against him and his celebrated reputation without your help."

He'd never needed her at his side before. Now he did. Kyra thought she knew why. From the beginning of their association, when David had come to work for him, Big Jim had viewed the bright, part-Navajo attorney as a young buck challenging his suzerainty, even while he'd considered him an asset. He'd betrayed as much without admitting it in so many words during their phone conversations shortly before she'd returned to Flag for her summer break and met David in person.

When they'd begun to see each other, the issue of David's Navajo background—doubtless buried in her father's psyche from the outset, despite his claim that a person's ethnic background didn't matter to him—had reared its ugly head. He'd all but admitted it mattered the earth when he'd confided that he didn't want "Navajo grandchildren."

Now David was a celebrated private attorney, known for making mincemeat of prosecutors and slick corporate defense lawyers. Simultaneously, with retirement looming, Big Jim had lost his edge. Though she hated to admit that, Kyra couldn't help but sense it. While he genuinely respected her experience and listened to her advice, he wanted her to come back for this trial to rattle David with her presence, she thought. Give himself a boost.

Notwithstanding her dislike of being used and her nagging sense that Paul Naminga was innocent despite the evidence against him, she was Big Jim's daughter. She was on his side. If it could be avoided, she didn't want to see him go down in flames on his last case.

She squeezed his hand. "I'll talk to Jonathan about it," she offered, referring to her boss, U.S. Attorney Jonathan Hargrave. "Maybe we can work something out. If I went back to Kansas City now, and worked for a month or so, maybe he'd let me return for a couple of weeks when the trial comes up."

As it turned out, Kyra's boss had been about to call her with a similar proposal. One of her fellow assistants had been diagnosed with chronic fatigue syndrome and would be out of the office for an indefinite period. Another had resigned suddenly when her husband was transferred to Singapore. Given the fact that its staff was shorthanded already, the Kansas City U.S. Attorney's Office was operating in crisis mode.

"Has the trial you're involved with gotten started yet?" he asked anxiously. "If not, maybe you could give me a couple of weeks...head up our team in the McMullen case. As you know, we'll be getting a couple of new people soon. I'd have no problem at all with you returning to Arizona once *U.S. v. McMullen* has been put to bed."

The situation was tailor-made. Kyra could help her father when he needed her most while temporarily avoiding the heartrending probability of running into David every which way she turned. She could fly up and rent a car, leaving the Cherokee in her father's driveway.

"That would suit me perfectly, Jon," she answered. "The trial here's been put on hold for six weeks. My return to Kansas City won't inconvenience anyone."

* * *

David learned of Kyra's absence a week later from Big Jim's secretary, Jody Ann Daniels, when he stopped by the courthouse to file some papers.

"You'll never guess who flew the coop," she confided, her curiosity about what David's reaction would be clearly evident.

Kyra, I suppose, he thought, doing his best to keep his face expressionless. On the verge of phoning her at her father's house to ask if they could meet somewhere and talk, he was keenly disappointed to learn that she was out of reach.

Somewhat blandly, he voiced his speculation.

Jody dimpled with pleasure. "Good guess."

"Where'd she go?" he asked, unable to evince a total lack of interest in Kyra's whereabouts.

"Back to K.C. for some important case."

David was silent a moment, letting the idea settle. "So...she won't be here to help her father when the Naminga trial starts?" he said at last.

The secretary's smile broadened. *"Au contraire,"* she said in her usual teasing manner. "She's supposed to be back a few days before it gets underway."

He'd have to do without Kyra, it seemed, for approximately five weeks. Meanwhile his inner man was crying out for her touch. I'd settle for the chance just to hold her, he thought as he bade Jody goodbye and headed down the stairs.

He was thinking about the figures in the sand painting his great-grandfather had made, and was unenthusiastically removing a can of chili from the cupboard that evening when Suzy Horvath called, inviting him to supper at her house.

"With Kyra away, I thought you might like some company," she said hopefully. "I've got some baby back ribs in the freezer and a powerhouse mesquite recipe…"

David had tasted her mesquite ribs before. And they were a damned sight better than the canned chili he was about to heat. He was also very lonely. "All right," he agreed at last, "provided it's on a 'just friends' basis."

Suzy was silent for a moment. "Okay by me," she said at last. "I'm nothing if not patient."

Agreeing to present himself at her house in an hour, David headed for his bedroom to shower and change. If Suzy was intimating Kyra and he were an item again, she probably knew they'd spent a couple of nights together on the reservation, he thought. Hell, the whole town probably knew it. He wouldn't put it past Jim Frakes to have asked Red Miner's deputies and the Navajo police to be on the lookout for them, if he thought there was the slightest chance they would be intimate.

Suzy welcomed him at her front door with a peck on the cheek and a friendly hug that made him decidedly uncomfortable. Though Kyra didn't seem to remember the words they'd spoken in the gorge, he did. He considered them pledged to each other.

They kept the conversation light as he watched her rustle around in the kitchen and they sat down to eat. It was only after they'd finished the ribs, which were delicious, that Suzy lapsed into a long silence, then confronted him on the topic that seemed to interest her most.

"I know I shouldn't ask," she admitted, her exquisitely lacquered nails tracing a nervous pattern on the tablecloth. "But we've been friends for a long time. And I have a personal interest at stake."

He waited, his silence inviting her to continue though he'd have preferred to be anywhere else on earth at the moment.

"I was wondering if you're serious about Kyra," she

blurted after a slight hesitation. "Or just indulging in a reprise of what happened between you five years ago."

Reluctant to hurt her, David wasn't sure how to answer. If he told her they were man and wife...that they were married in the Little Colorado Canyon by his dead great-grandfather a couple of weeks ago, she would think he was out of his head, he thought. Yet it would be cruel to give her any reason to hope.

"I'm going to marry her," he said at last. "That is, if she'll have me. The fact is, I'm crazy wild in love with her. Unfortunately, I can't seem to get to first base."

Retreating into her famous poise, Suzy appeared both envious and disbelieving. "She's a fool if that's true," she said emphatically. "I may be prejudiced. But I think you're one heck of a guy...the kind any woman in her right mind would want."

At home in her Kansas City, Missouri, condo a few days before her scheduled return to Flagstaff, Kyra was flipping through the November and December pages in her date book in order to mark down some future court dates her boss had handed her earlier that afternoon, when it was as if a light had suddenly switched on in her head. Her period was more than a month late. And she was usually as regular as clockwork.

I *can't* be pregnant, she told herself in the stunned moments that followed. It's just not possible! I've never made love to anyone but Brad. And our marriage ended three years ago.

Abruptly the dream she'd had just before awakening in her Cherokee near the rim of the Little Colorado, which had continued to haunt her, came into sharper focus. In it, she and David had been married by his dead great-grandfather in a traditional Navajo ceremony. Afterward, they'd gone to a hogan built a short distance from the others and consummated their vows.

That the scenario *was* a dream and didn't represent reality, she had little doubt. It was just too far-fetched to be an approximation of the truth. I suppose it's possible we made love in the Cherokee and my subconscious transformed the whole thing into something more special, more acceptable, wiping away the sordid memory of what really happened, she thought.

But she couldn't get herself to believe it. To take her that way and leave her to her own devices afterward would be too callous, even for David to contemplate.

Maybe she had some reproduction-related illness. The thing to do was to see her gynecologist at once. Worried and shaken, she looked up his office number in her personal directory and wrote it in large numerals on a piece of notepaper.

After a thorough examination, Kyra's gynecologist gave her the news. She was six or seven weeks pregnant. He was sure of his diagnosis.

Clearly unaware of her divorce three years earlier, he offered her his congratulations and asked that she convey them to her husband.

Her head spinning at the turn of events, Kyra didn't know what to think. Her initial surge of unreasoning joy was riddled with incredulity, followed by confusion. Later that morning, after walking aimlessly in the environs of the gynecologist's office, she phoned a friend, Miriam Kahn, who was a clinical psychologist, and asked if they could meet for lunch.

Over salads and Perrier at a popular local bistro, she poured out the whole incredible tale. "Do you think David returned from the gorge and made love to me in the Cherokee and then just left me in the lurch?" she asked, a keen sense of betrayal reverberating in her voice. "That I made up the dream about the gorge, the tribal gathering and the ceremony to cushion myself from a second abandonment? What I dreamed can't be real. His great-grandfather's *dead*, for God's sake!"

Miriam didn't have a ready answer. She thoughtfully pointed out that David had asked when he'd see Kyra again before she drove away from his grandmother's hogan. "That doesn't sound like the question of a man who's got betrayal or abandonment on his mind," she observed.

"So...what's the explanation?" Kyra asked. "Am I suffering from amnesia? According to my gynecologist, I'm definitely pregnant."

Her friend shrugged. "True amnesia is rare, but it's always a possibility. You can hardly ascribe what happened to time travel, after all. I know...quantum physics says that the past, present and future coexist, like pearls on a string. To my knowledge, though, no one's scientifically documented a way to jump from one to another."

Kyra pushed her salad away. She couldn't eat another bite. "If I have amnesia, what do you think caused it?" she asked.

Again Miriam shrugged. "You tell me."

She was silent a moment. "Maybe I just don't want to admit I had sex with David," she answered doubtfully.

At that, her friend raised an eyebrow. "You're saying that your dream, as you call it, may be a disowned, partially repressed memory?"

"I guess so. Is there some way I can find out?"

Miriam hesitated, obviously wary of handing out psychological advice to friends. "You could try hypnosis with a qualified professional," she suggested at last. "But that may not be necessary. Why don't your ask your partner in the canyon fantasy to recount his memories of what occurred?"

Unwilling that David should learn of her pregnancy until she could come to terms with what really had happened between them, Kyra tried to accept the notion that they'd made love in the Cherokee. Barring time travel, as her friend had pointed out, there wasn't any other logical explanation. It was entirely possible that she'd created the canyon dream to keep from having to face her own irresponsible behavior.

Overwhelmed by what had happened, and increasingly uncertain of her ability to tell fact from fiction, she took the rest of the afternoon off and headed home to begin packing for her return to Flagstaff. Goose bumps skittered down her arms when she pushed the message button on her answering machine and David's disembodied voice floated into her living room.

"Hello, Kyra," he'd recorded onto the machine's erasable tape. "I guess you're not at home. The Naminga trial's about to start. When are you coming back?" A short pause followed, as if he'd thought she might pick up after all. When she hadn't, he'd added in a tone like no other she'd heard from him, "I really need to talk to you."

When she didn't return his call, David spent the evening missing her. He had other problems, as well. Used to winning the legal battles he picked, he didn't take clients unless he believed strongly in their innocence. Yet, though he'd dredged up every bit of testimony he could find that would help Paul Naminga, he still didn't have a winning case. Unless he could come up with Ben Monongye's real killer, Paul would be sent to state prison, like his brother Leonard before him, for a crime he didn't commit.

Though so far it hadn't done him much good, he'd settled on Dale Cargill from among the victim's many enemies for a second look. A misfit member of a respected local family, Dale had been vociferously aggrieved when Ben had received a lucrative highway construction contract he'd wanted for himself as the result of a federal law favoring minority-run companies. He'd accused Ben of price-fixing in the hearing of several witnesses and—while inebriated in a public place—physically threatened him.

Further, Dale's role as the owner of the supposedly stolen car in the *Leonard* Naminga case had always troubled him. Dale's assertion that he'd gone out to the parking lot of the Red Rock Tavern and found his car missing had never been substantiated.

Unfortunately, all he had was a hunch. It wasn't enough to support a demand that Dale submit to DNA testing on the theory that the dyed Caucasian hair found by crime-scene specialists in Ben's dressing room belonged to him.

Searching her face when he picked her up at the Flagstaff airport, Kyra's dad worried aloud about her drawn, preoccupied expression. "Is everything okay with you, gal?" he asked.

In spite of the pitched battle she was waging with herself over what, if anything, to tell David about her pregnancy, she assured Big Jim that everything was fine. "The prosecution's ready, your honor," she quipped.

Relieved, Big Jim gave Kyra the disquieting news that Sheriff Miner's wife, Flossie, had suffered a mild heart attack during her absence. "She's on the mend," he reassured when Kyra questioned him about Flossie's prognosis. "I'm sure she'd love some company."

Deeply fond of the cozy, down-to-earth, sheriff's wife, Kyra visited her at the hospital that afternoon. Giving Flossie a big bouquet of yellow roses and a warm kiss on the cheek, she pulled up a chair and demanded to know the latest prognosis. To her relief, Flossie had a good chance of leading a normal life after her discharge. She'd be going home in a few days.

"Of course, I'll have to eat a fat- and salt-free diet from now on," Flossie acknowledged, making a face.

Reassured that the older woman would be all right, Kyra told her a little about her on-again, off-again relationship with David, though she didn't share the news about her pregnancy or the conundrum that was troubling her. Unfortunately, Flossie didn't have a chance to comment after Dale Cargill and his mother arrived for a brief visit, bearing a box of Flossie's favorite chocolates.

After they'd gone, with Betty Cargill promising to return in a moment, Kyra didn't revisit the subject. Instead, she remarked that Dale looked different. "His hair seems darker than it did the night we all had dinner at my father's house," she noted.

At that, Flossie laughed outright. "He dyes it. Didn't you know?"

Kyra thought instantly of the dyed Caucasian hair that had been found in Ben Monongye's dressing room. Horrified, since she'd known the Cargills, including Dale, all her life, she tried to tell herself the hair could have been sloughed off in the rental trailer by someone unconnected with the murder weeks earlier. Besides, even if it did belong to Dale, it doesn't prove he killed Ben, she thought. Just that he was present at some point.

Her sense that Dale *was* the killer grew, just by the feel of it. She was taut as piano wire with the thought when Dale's mother walked in, bidding them each a warm renewed hello, and settled down for a chat.

At last, Kyra couldn't take the tension any longer. Kissing Flossie's cheek and promising to visit again soon, she bade the sheriff's wife and Dale's mother a somewhat hurried goodbye and rushed to her Cherokee, which she'd left in the hospital parking lot.

As she got behind the wheel, another epiphany gripped her by the throat. Over her father's dinner table on the night she'd mentioned to Flossie, Betty Cargill had revealed that Dale had kept a diary since high school. If certain senators who came readily to mind had been foolish enough to jot down every detail of their private lives, including episodes of wrongdoing, mightn't Dale, who was no genius, have done likewise?

What if he chronicled Ben's murder in his own handwriting? she thought with a little shudder, the hair standing up on the back of her neck.

By itself, telling a judge that Dale dyed his hair might not be enough to compel a DNA test. Or get Red Miner's deputies a search warrant. The history of Dale's feud with Ben Monongye over the construction project he'd lost to the minority contractor at a time when Dale's business was in financial trouble would have to be laid out in detail, and that would take time—enough time for Dale to bury the missing murder weapon and destroy any other physical evidence that was still in his possession.

If she could find the diaries before that happened...

The possibility that she could solve the case and exonerate Paul Naminga pushed all thought of her pregnancy from her head. Taking a moment to sort things out, she recalled that during their conversation in Flossie's hospital room, Betty Cargill had mentioned Dale would be tied up in a county planning commission meeting, trying to get one of his proposed construction projects approved, most of the afternoon. If the commissioners proceeded at their usual pace, he'd be stuck for several hours, at least.

It might be their only chance. She had to phone David, she thought, her adrenaline flowing. He was going to be blown away. Besides, she wanted backup. She was dialing his home number on her cellular phone as she exited the hospital parking lot.

David's secretary, a middle-aged Navajo woman, answered on the second ring. "I'm sorry, Mrs. Martin, but he's not here," she said in response to Kyra's request to talk to him. "He left for Prescott maybe two and a half hours ago. If it's important that you talk with him now, you can reach him on his cellular phone."

Suddenly feeling very alone in what she proposed to do, Kyra dialed David's mobile number at the next traffic light. To her relief, he picked up right away.

"David, this is Kyra," she began.

Pleasure burst into being in his voice. "You're back!" he exclaimed. "When am I going to see you?"

"This afternoon, I hope. I'd like some backup if possible."

Ready to give her whatever she wanted, David wasn't sure what she was talking about.

"Darlin'..." he began, letting the single word trail off into a question.

Kyra knew he'd considered Dale, too, having thoroughly discussed the case with him. She felt certain he'd driven to Prescott to talk with a former construction supervisor Dale had fired six months earlier. Supposedly the man had witnessed an altercation between Dale and the victim.

Before David could respond, she was leapfrogging ahead. "I'm almost sure I know who the killer is," she informed him excitedly. "*Dale Cargill*. In addition to having been one of Ben Monongye's worst enemies, he dyes his hair black...the color of the hair Red Miner's deputies found in Ben's trailer. There's more. At least, I hope there is. According to his mother, Dale has kept a diary since high school. We've got to get our hands on the one he was working on at the time of the murder!"

Chapter Eleven

Parked in his truck outside the construction project where Dale's ex-foreman worked, David had just finished interviewing him. He'd gleaned a wealth of background detail about the feud between Dale and Ben Monongye—enough that he believed he was on the right track. Now *Kyra* had phoned. She was back within reach. He wanted to hug her so tightly that both their bones would break.

"Babe," he said with a little shake of his head, his voice full of relief, pride and a deep affection she was too charged up to interpret, "you may have saved Paul. Dale's topped my suspect list for weeks...."

Static on the line drowned out her answer. Meanwhile, a disquieting thought had occurred to him.

"What did you mean about needing *backup?*" he demanded worriedly. "Surely you're not thinking of searching his house. If Dale killed Ben, as we believe, he's extremely dangerous. Besides, we still have a constitution in this country. You can't just walk into someone's house without a search warrant and collect evidence. Anything you gained that way would be ruled inadmissible…''

"Not if my purpose is stopping by to ask him over for dinner. If I happen to stumble across something pertinent while I'm there…'' She let the phrase dangle. "I won't remove any evidence. Just look around. I *can* testify to what I stumbled across while I was waiting for him, can't I? If we go through channels and he hears via the grapevine that you've been focusing on him, he may get worried and destroy the diary that incriminates him.''

Though there was continued static on their connection, David managed to catch most of what she'd said. His alarm grew to staggering proportions. "I categorically refuse to let you go out there,'' he said, all but shouting to be heard.

Abruptly the static cleared.

"I'm not afraid of Dale,'' Kyra responded, attempting to ignore a little shudder she couldn't suppress. "It won't be a problem if his front door is locked. I know where the spare key is kept. If he comes home early and catches me, I'll hear his tires on the gravel. He'll find me sitting in the living room reading a magazine when he walks in. He won't suspect a thing. Frakeses and Cargills have been making themselves at home in each other's houses for years. Matter of fact, he'll probably try to flirt with me.''

He thought he could detect a note of false bravado in her voice. "Kyra, I won't have it!'' he ordered. "You're not to go in that house without me, do you hear? Or anywhere near it. I'm leaving now. I'll meet you at Molly's Bar and Grill and we'll decide what to do. That's twenty minutes from Dale's place. Promise me you'll wait.''

She knew as well as he did that he was an hour-and-a-half's drive from Flag, even if he took the Interstate. And that didn't include the subsequent trip east to Dale's house. If the meeting let out early, they'd lose their chance.

During the ensuing argument, David managed to wring a promise from her that she'd wait for him until 2:30 p.m., at least. "I'll be there if I have to fly without wings," he promised. "Please, babe. Don't do anything to put your pretty hide in danger."

Parking near Molly's as promised around 2 p.m., Kyra nervously checked her watch. She felt certain David wouldn't arrive in time to accompany her. It'll be just my luck if I wait around here and the meeting lets out early, she thought. Or maybe the matter that interested Dale will be tabled. The chance to exonerate Paul will then vanish like a puff of smoke.

Unwilling to let that happen, she decided to wait until two-thirty and not a minute longer. Dale wasn't going to get away with murder if she could help it.

The appointed time came and went without any sign of David's truck. In the meantime, if its schedule hadn't changed, the planning commission meeting would have gotten underway roughly an hour and a half earlier. She didn't have the faintest idea where Dale's item had been placed on the agenda.

Another ten minutes passed. Picking up her cellular phone, Kyra started to dial David's mobile number again, then thought better of it. If she reached him, he'd only put more pressure on her to wait.

Instead, she called the county offices and asked one of the building and planning department secretaries if the meeting was still in session. Learning that it was, she decided somewhat nervously to go ahead. Even if he'd already concluded his business, Dale might not go straight home, she tried to tell herself. He might run by his office first. Or stop off for a drink someplace. From what she'd heard since returning to Flagstaff, he was seriously abusing alcohol.

Less than real to her, despite her gynecologist's insistence that there could be no mistake, the fact of her pregnancy didn't enter her head. It simply didn't occur to her that she could be putting the vulnerable new life inside her in mortal danger.

Burning up the pavement in his effort to prevent Kyra from going to Dale's house alone, David was frustrated by a "gapers' block" of slower traffic that had formed south of an accident in the interstate's northbound lanes. Already hampered by a tight time frame, he wasn't going to make it. If he knew Kyra, she'd go without him, he thought.

For some reason, as he crept forward, her feat in accessing the past the afternoon she'd appeared in the gorge came to mind, and he realized it held a lesson for him. If she could do what she did without any training or practice, he should be able to travel to her side. God knew the need was great enough.

Just then the "gapers' block" eased, and traffic resumed its normal speed. He decided to drive as fast as he could to the restaurant and bar, where she might still be waiting for him. If she wasn't there, he'd turn to extraordinary measures.

A bachelor, Dale lived alone in the former Cargill family home on several all-but-treeless acres adjacent to his construction company's equipment compound. His parents had retired, turned the business over to him and moved to a new, ranch-style residence in town near the country club. His truck wasn't anywhere in sight.

Though the front door was locked, the key was exactly where Kyra expected to find it, beneath some overturned clay flowerpots that had been shoved partway beneath the front porch, and she let herself in. The interior, which was decorated in nondescript fifties style, smelled stale, as if it could use a good airing. To her disgust, the drapes and overstuffed chairs in the living room exuded Dale's sweaty, insecure scent.

Hunting for the murder weapon, which he'd surely hidden if it was still in his possession, could take hours, she realized. With an undetermined amount of time at her disposal, she decided to look for his diaries first.

She found them almost at once. Conveniently arrayed in plain sight, the motley collection of spiral notebooks was jammed onto several dusty shelves in a former bedroom he'd converted to a home office.

Unfortunately, though the dates they chronicled were scrawled in ink on their front covers, they weren't arranged in chronological order. Searching frantically through them while she kept one ear cocked for the sound of an approaching vehicle, she couldn't seem to find the notebook that covered the period of Ben's death.

Arriving at the pickup-jammed parking lot outside Molly's, David found to his dismay that Kyra had already left. A quick phone call to the county building department only compounded his worry. The planning commission meeting had let out five minutes earlier. Unless he stopped at one of his favorite watering holes, Dale would probably head straight home. If his ex-foreman was to be believed, there weren't any construction jobs vying for his attention.

Her blithe assumption that she'd hear him coming up the drive notwithstanding, it was all too likely that he'd catch Kyra unawares, going through his things. I've got to get to her...*now!* he thought. Before it's too late. Twenty minutes could make all the difference.

Despite his native proficiency and the formidable gift of his great-grandfather's tutelage, his ability to employ the shamanic secrets of time travel had proven spotty, at best. At the museum grounds he'd failed twice to step back into the past and review events with an eye to proving his client's innocence.

He could only try. Resting his hands on his knees and shutting his eyes, he focused on the ancient chant, the immersion of self in the power that suffused the universe. If he could pull it off, he'd be able to collapse time and arrive at her side in what would have been the past if he were forced to travel there by the usual means.

At Dale's house, just a minute or two had passed. Kyra was still going through the diaries when she heard a crunch of gravel outside that sounded like footsteps. Chills of fear rippled through her. Maybe Dale had returned, seen her Cherokee parked outside his house and left his truck by the mailbox, approaching quietly on foot to peer in the window. If he had a guilty conscience, as seemed likely, he might be very suspicious about her presence.

Her heart beating wildly, she made it to the living room just before the front door opened. To her relief and amazement, *David* was standing there.

Flying into his arms, she retreated self-consciously. "I thought you were Dale returning," she gasped. "You can't possibly have come on foot. Where's your truck? I didn't hear it approach."

David was no Cargill family friend, and for him it was definitely breaking and entering to be there in Dale's living room without his permission. Yet his relief at finding Kyra unharmed pushed any such concerns into the background. Despite the fact that she'd withdrawn from him almost immediately, the way she'd run to him had warmed his heart.

"My truck refused to start in Molly's parking lot," he said.

"Then…how'd you get here?"

"I stuck out my thumb and a speed demon of a semi driver took pity on me. Have you found anything yet?"

Kyra shook her head regretfully. "I've checked all the diaries in his study. The one that would bring the collection up-to-date…and cover Ben's murder…isn't to be found."

"The planning commission let out—" he checked his watch "—ten minutes ago. Even if Dale was forced to wait until the bitter end, that gives us another ten minutes at best."

Little shivers ran down her spine. "Unless he hangs around to lobby someone," she said briskly. "Or stops for a couple of beers. I haven't looked inside his desk yet. Maybe that's where his current diary is kept."

A quick search of Dale's desk drawers left them empty-handed. "If he chronicled the murder in one of these note-books, he's probably burned it," David speculated, wiping away their fingerprints with his handkerchief. "Or hidden it someplace."

Kyra was thoughtful. "Maybe not," she said slowly. "If I were keeping a diary, I'd jot down the day's events just before I turned in for the night. Let's check his bedroom."

It would be difficult to make the argument that Kyra had absently picked up Dale's current journal while waiting for him in his living room if it was usually kept in his bedroom. Yet both she and David were committed now. Convinced that Dale had killed a man, and that an innocent might go to prison for it, they agreed to search now and do whatever fast-talking was necessary later.

Kyra couldn't help letting out a little screech of delight when they found the notebook they sought quite easily inside Dale's bedside table. Breathlessly flipping through the pages, they located the entry they sought. She moved a little closer to David as they scanned Dale's account of the crime that had been committed at the dance festival and craft fair.

Too bad everyone who thinks I'm an incompetent, lame-brained disappointment to my parents, who won't be able to keep the family construction company afloat, didn't see the way I seized my chance to get rid of Ben Monongye this afternoon. Thanks to my courage and quick thinking, they'll have to let bids on the Route 89A project again. This time, I'll win. And keep the company from being flushed down the toilet.

When I saw the fight between Ben and Paul Naminga, and then that Navajo brat pleading with Paul for help, I knew what I had to do. With nearly everyone already assembled at the stage and viewing stands, it was easy to slip into Paul's trailer, put on his costume, catch Ben before he emerged from his and then put the costume back where it belonged.

Luckily I had my hunting knife in my pocket. I wish I could tell somebody what happened. Share my cleverness with them.

The narrative went on to touch on Dale's enmity toward Paul as well. He described himself as "glad" that Paul would be blamed for the act he'd committed.

Amazing how I managed to get two for the price of one. Though it happened five years ago, the Hopi bastard won't let the matter of his brother's conviction rest. He keeps trying to find evidence that I and not that lush, Leonard Naminga, killed those old people. Cooling his heels in prison ought to put a stop to his digging for a while.

The rest of the day's entry was a polemic against set-asides for minority business owners.

David and Kyra looked at each other. Maybe Dale had run into the older couple who'd died after his car had plowed into theirs. It made perfect sense, in light of their discovery. It was anybody's guess how poor, drunken Leonard Naminga had stumbled into the situation.

"We've got Dale dead to rights on Ben, at least," David said, "provided we can think of someplace to hide this notebook in the house until we can subpoena it for evidence."

Kyra thought a moment. "Why not in plain sight... among his other diaries?" she asked.

He shook his head. "You couldn't make a case for finding it there without the defense arguing it was gained by breaking and entering...and therefore inadmissible as evidence."

"Then let's put it between the magazines in that stack in the living room. Even if he misses it and starts searching, he's not likely to find it there right away. While he's driving himself crazy with worry, we'll be phoning the sheriff."

David nodded. "Let's do it then. And get the hell out of here."

They'd just managed to hide the notebook and place another that closely resembled it in the nightstand beside Dale's bed when the crunch of tires on gravel and a cloud of dust approaching from the highway announced his arrival.

Though he'd probably accept Kyra's presence, David's meant they'd have some powerful explaining to do. Neither of them had a gun or any type of weapon to use in self-defense.

"Get out of the house...quick!" Kyra ordered, taking

charge of the situation, though her knees were on the verge of buckling. "There's a wash fringed with cottonwoods about half a mile west of here. The highway crosses it. Cut through the scrub. When I can get free of Dale, I'll meet you there."

Predictably, David refused to budge. "And leave you here with a confessed murderer?" he asked. "No damn way."

The cloud of gravel dust was drawing closer.

"You *have* to go," she urged. "Or he'll shoot us both. He carries a shotgun in his truck."

Realizing that she was probably right, David reluctantly agreed to sneak out the back door and head for the wash while Kyra distracted Dale. In fact, he planned to hide outside the house until she'd made her escape. He loved her. And they were pledged to each other. Whatever had caused her to refuse him after their night in the gorge, he would be her protector.

He'd barely left when Dale braked in front of the porch with a little sputter of gravel and turned off his truck's engine. By the time he walked into the house, Kyra was seated in the least repulsive of his easy chairs, leafing through a magazine. Though her heart was pounding, she set the magazine aside with a smile and got to her feet.

"Hi," she said casually. "I've been waiting for you."

Perhaps because of his guilty secret, Dale regarded her skeptically for a moment. "I saw your Cherokee when I came up the lane," he said. "What gives?"

"I had to drive out to the Brady place to interview a witness for Dad. On the way back, I decided to stop and ask you to supper. We've seen so little of each other since I've returned to Flagstaff."

The look on his face told her he wanted to believe her, but hadn't quite managed it yet.

"When you weren't home, I realized you were still at the planning commission meeting," she explained. "I was thirsty, so I let myself in for a drink of water. And decided to wait for you. I hope that was okay...."

The tension drained visibly from Dale's face. A fatuous smile replaced it as he took off his bifocals and laid them on the TV console.

"You know it's *always* okay for you to come out and see me, Kyra," he said, gripping her upper arms with his damp, beefy hands. "I've been crazy about you since you were in high school."

He was going to kiss her. Kyra wasn't sure she could bear it without throwing up. She was saved by a sudden noise behind the house that electrified them both.

Oh, no! she thought. *David didn't leave.* He hung around to protect me.

Meanwhile, Dale's expression had changed to one of suspicion again. "Hang on, honey, while I see what's happening out back," he shouted grimly, running out to his truck for the shotgun.

"I'm sure it was just a jackrabbit," Kyra pleaded to no avail when he came back inside and started down the bedroom hall.

She wasn't sure whether to make a run for it or hang around in case she could be of help to David. Though she removed the keys to the Cherokee from her purse and clutched them tightly in the palm of her right hand, just in case, she decided on the latter course.

To her relief, Dale returned to the living room a moment later without having found the source of the disturbance. "I told you it was a jackrabbit, Dale," she said as sweetly as she could, edging toward the door. "Will 7 p.m. be okay? For dinner, I mean."

"What's your rush?" he replied. "I just got here."

Seconds later he was covering her mouth with a sloppy, wet kiss. Withdrawing from it, Kyra pretended shyness, a touch of embarrassment.

"Dale, please!" she protested, hoping the pink in her cheeks would be mistaken for a romantic blush. "We haven't even dated…yet. I've got to go home and cook for you. Did I mention that Dad will be playing cards with the boys at Red Miner's tonight?"

Clearly tantalized by her hint of intimacy to come, Dale let her go with obvious reluctance. Though she was shaking inside, Kyra snatched the opportunity to edge out the door and slide behind the wheel of her Cherokee.

"See you later, okay? I'm glad you could accept my invitation," she said with a friendly smile, starting the engine and turning her vehicle around before he could change his mind and press her to stay. With all her heart she prayed the noise they'd heard meant David had left the premises.

As she exited the gravel drive and turned west on the highway, toward Flagstaff, David was running for his life toward the wash, which cut across the Cargill property before passing through a culvert beneath the highway at the spot Kyra had indicated. Meanwhile, nervous in retrospect about what she might have seen while she was waiting for him, Dale had gone straight to his bedroom to confirm his current diary's presence.

It appeared to be exactly where he'd left it, though without his bifocals he couldn't make out the inscription on its cover. Seconds later, the view from his bedroom window—that of David Yazzie running toward Cinco Wash—grabbed his attention and sent him racing for his shotgun again.

He couldn't get off an accurate shot without his glasses. In the process of snatching them up, he dropped them, causing one of the lenses to pop out of its frame. Swearing, he tossed them aside and ran out the back door.

A bumbler at many things, Dale wasn't a crack shot. Unfortunately for David, that day he had a measure of luck. The shot he aimed at the part-Navajo defense attorney as the latter dived for the protection of the wash hit him in the shoulder. Though it was a graze rather than a serious wound, the pain was excruciating.

Parking on the verge of the highway just beyond the wash where Dale couldn't see her from the house, Kyra was dialing her cellular phone when she heard the shotgun being fired. David *can't* be hurt, she thought frantically, craning her neck.

A moment later her father answered on his private office line. "Dad," she said urgently, "I'm on my way back to Flag. I've just learned that Dale Cargill is Ben Monongye's killer. Yes, I know he's a family friend. But it happens to be the truth."

Her father didn't say anything for a moment.

"I was waiting for him at his house to ask him over for dinner and I happened to pick up one of his diaries to pass the time. It recounts his murder of Ben in detail, in his own handwriting," she continued. "I hid it in a pile of magazines when he showed up. Considering what I'd learned, I felt fortunate to get out of his house in one piece."

Frantic over the gun blast she'd heard, she decided on the spur of the moment not to tell Big Jim about David's part in finding the diary. She and David hadn't compared stories yet.

"I think Dale's become suspicious that I saw something," she finished. "If you want the evidence...and I know you do, because you'd never knowingly prosecute an innocent man...you'd better get Red Miner to send out a chopper with some of his deputies."

Silence continued to greet her assertion for a moment. "You're not kidding, are you, gal?" her father said at last. "You come on home. I'll have Red send out the deputies like you suggest. Hank Beamish happens to be in his office down the hall. He'll give them a search warrant."

Flipping her phone shut with a terse "See you later," Kyra was about to get out of the Cherokee and look for David when he emerged from the cottonwoods clutching his left arm. There was blood on his shirt. Aghast, she held open the passenger door for him.

"Please...tell me you're not badly hurt," she beseeched him.

Taking off the shirt, he wrapped it around his arm to stanch the bleeding. "The wound's superficial," he grunted. "I trust you called the sheriff."

Chapter Twelve

On their return to Flagstaff, Kyra took David straight to the emergency room. The nurse who screened patients for the seriousness of their cases ushered him inside immediately after seeing the blood on his shirt and the ragged gash one of Dale's shots had opened in his upper arm.

When she started to follow him through the large, automatic glass doors that separated the medical area from the waiting room, the woman demanded her credentials. "Are you his wife?" she asked. "Or a relative?"

"I'm...er, just an acquaintance," Kyra replied in embarrassment.

"Then I'm afraid you'll have to wait here."

The look on David's face as he was ushered inside for treatment told her she'd only wounded him further. Well, what was she *supposed* to say? she asked herself as she settled down to wait with a dog-eared magazine. That she was madly in love with him, but that they had no future unless he confessed to the way he'd betrayed her five years ago? That was nobody's business but their own.

It was only a half hour later, when a heavily pregnant woman passed through the hall, clutching at her stomach as her husband leaned solicitously over her, that Kyra remembered her own, less advanced but similar state. Though it was still difficult for her to believe—or even remember— that she was carrying David's child, given the fact that she couldn't clearly recall the circumstances of its conception, she was overcome with remorse and self-loathing.

The tiny being who's dependent on me for life itself could have been injured or even killed, thanks to my reckless behavior, she excoriated herself. How could I have been so irresponsible? So thoughtless? Abruptly sick to her stomach, she rushed into a nearby rest room, vomited into one of the toilets and bent over a sink to splash cold water on her face.

David had returned to the waiting room by the time she emerged with a washed-out look and a sour taste lingering in her mouth.

"What's wrong?" he asked immediately, clearly feeling much better as he got to his feet and slipped his good arm about her shoulders. "You look like you've seen a ghost."

She withdrew a little, on principle. "It was just a delayed reaction to what happened, I guess. If you're feeling up to it, let's go over to my dad's office and see if he has any news about Dale's arrest."

His blue eyes assessed her. "Okay," he said at last. "You'll have to drive. My truck's at Molly's, remember? Plus they gave me a pain shot."

We'll have some powerful explaining to do when we show up together, Kyra realized as they headed for the parking lot. Somehow, we've got to explain our mutual presence at Dale's without seeming to have gone there specifically to search for evidence.

Big Jim was suspicious the moment she arrived in David's company. "I might have known you'd be mixed up in this somehow," he said disapprovingly, declining to greet David by name. "According to one of Red Miner's deputies, Dale claims you were skulking around the back of his house after Kyra left. Want to tell me what you were doing there?"

David was nothing if not accustomed to thinking on his feet. Besides, he'd been mulling over a potentially truthful but less-than-revealing answer since leaving the hospital.

"I was in Prescott when Kyra phoned and mentioned she might be stopping by Dale's place," he responded in a calm, straightforward manner. "I tried to talk her out of it. The fact is, Dale's topped my list of suspects for weeks. Naturally, she refused to take my advice. So I drove like hell as far as Molly's Bar and Grill, where I had trouble with my pickup. I stuck out my thumb and a semi driver took me the rest of the way."

Big Jim considered his answer for a moment. "So...you hung around outside the house to make sure Kyra was okay? Is that it?" he asked.

David nodded.

"Well," the aging prosecutor admitted, "I have to thank you for it."

It seemed David was home free, at least for the moment. Meanwhile, Kyra still had some explaining to do. She was also dying to know whether Dale had found and destroyed the incriminating diary before Red Miner's deputies could descend on his house.

Instead of pretending she'd found the telltale notebook in Dale's living room, which he was certain to deny, she decided to tell a closer approximation of the truth, even if that meant a reprimand from Judge Beamish. If she could convince him she'd discovered it out of idle curiosity, rather than in the course of searching for clues, the diary should remain admissible as evidence.

"Has Dale been arrested? Have they found the diary?" she asked before her father could turn the spotlight of his suspicion on her.

"Yes to both questions," he answered. "You said on the phone that you were waiting for him at his house so you could ask him to dinner. I find that somewhat hard to believe, considering the way you've always avoided him in the past. But we'll let that go for the moment. I want to know how you managed to stumble across the relevant notebook."

She glanced down at her feet, then back at her father's face. "The magazines in Dale's living room were boring," she said. "As you may recall, Betty Cargill told us about Dale's diaries over dinner at your house shortly after I returned to Flag. I know I shouldn't have gone looking for them. But I was curious."

He accepted her reply without comment—perhaps because he wanted to. "As we speak," he said, "Red Miner's deputies are combing Dale's house and property for the murder weapon." He turned to David. "I've asked Hank Beamish to sign an order for Paul Naminga's release. He should be free at any moment."

Kyra knew that David would want to be present when his client was released. "You'd better get over there," she told him. "Or you'll miss the big moment."

He nodded in agreement. "Come with me. He and Julie will want to see you, too. They'll want to thank you for the role you played in exonerating him."

She could feel her father watching her. Feel him thinking about the way David had deserted her in the past and asking himself if she'd give the part-Navajo attorney another chance. What will he say when he finds out I allowed David to get me pregnant? she wondered.

"If you don't mind, I'd rather not," she said. "I don't belong there. You do. Go on...enjoy your big moment."

Aware Paul would expect him, and conscious of the fact that she'd never open up and tell him what was keeping them apart in front of her father, he did as she asked.

Ten minutes later, Paul Naminga was a free man. With his wife, Julie, and David at his side, he answered reporters' questions on the sidewalk between the jail and the courthouse. Several TV cameras were present. It was beginning to look as if the story would be picked up by the national media.

Elated as he was that his client had been proven innocent, David couldn't help but feel he was losing his second chance with Kyra just as he'd lost the first. For Paul's sake, he managed to smile with a flash of strong, white teeth against his bronze complexion and offer several punchy sound bites when the ladies and gentlemen of the press demanded a statement.

Was it something I did? he wondered. Or something I *didn't* do? Whatever the case, Kyra has forgotten our vows and the love we made in the canyon of the Little Colorado.

Inundated by well-wishers, many of them paramedics who'd worked with Paul and Native Americans, Paul and Julie decided to throw a party at their home that evening to celebrate his release and exoneration. David seized the opportunity to phone Kyra and insist that she attend. "It's because of your courage and determination to get at the truth that Paul's free tonight," he said. "He and Julie want to thank you. It's only fair that you give them that chance."

With the same reluctance that had echoed in her voice earlier, Kyra agreed to put in a brief appearance. "You needn't pick me up," she answered when he offered. "I can drive myself."

She showed up halfway through the festivities, in time to see David talking with Suzy Horvath, who was avidly scribbling down quotes in one of her slender reporter's notebooks.

Avoiding them, Kyra made her way through the crush to offer the Namingas her congratulations. Somewhat embarrassed by it, she downplayed their effusive thanks. Moments later, David caught up with her as she slipped out of the spotlight to select a few munchies from the heavily laden buffet the Namingas' friends and neighbors had gotten together.

"We need to talk," he said, his deep voice compelling as he tugged at her hand. "Something's still wrong between us. I want to know what it is."

I'm carrying his baby, she mused, noting the callused texture of his palm as she let him lead her outside to an old-fashioned swing on the deserted front porch. And, she thought, the precious scrap of life she'd risked so foolishly that afternoon could have her eyes, his smile. Or vice versa.

Yet what was she supposed to tell him? That she wanted him to admit to taking her father's money in exchange for dumping her five years earlier? And apologize? If I have to elicit the words, she thought, they'll be meaningless. To count for anything, they'd have to come from him first.

Sitting down beside her on the swing, he set it gently in motion. "I want to know what's wrong between us," he reiterated.

"Why don't you tell me?" she answered, keeping the loving, warmhearted woman she was firmly out of reach.

Though they talked some more, she quickly sensed it was hopeless. He wasn't going to confess. If only the dream she'd had about reconciliation and a wedding in the gorge had substance, she lamented. She would be the happiest woman on earth.

"I know I should have said goodbye instead of leaving you hanging five years ago," he admitted, echoing the words he'd spoken at the little reservation motel. "And I've apologized for it. What more do you want?"

They were still moving in circles. Unable to take it any more, she got to her feet. If he wouldn't admit to taking the money without coaching, he wasn't going to tell her the truth about making love to her in the Cherokee and casually walking away, either. She needed more—a lot more than that if she was going raise a child with him. They needed a clean slate if they were ever to have a lasting relationship.

"I'm going home to spend some time with my dad since I'll be leaving for Kansas City at the end of the week," she said, dismissing his question.

A moment later he was watching her walk out of his life, headed for her Cherokee. Though it was a dry evening, he felt like a man standing in the rain without an umbrella.

Perverse as always, Kyra's heart sank when David didn't phone the following morning. Or the next. The days were ticking by. Soon it would be time for her to go. It seems he's taken me at my word, she thought. She had no way of knowing that he was *willing* her to stay, to remember what had happened between them, with all the strength he could muster.

Later that week a story appeared in the local paper about him taking on a high-profile case. He'd be representing a South Dakota tribe against large-scale development and mining interests. Sick at heart as she gazed at the photo of him that accompanied the piece, Kyra wasn't able to hold out any longer. She couldn't leave for Kansas City without making a final stab at setting things straight.

With a sudden flash of inspiration, she decided to visit David's grandmother. Each time she'd been in Mary Many Horses's presence, the older woman's wisdom and honesty had shone from her jet-dark eyes and wrinkled face. Maybe she could offer some advice.

It was a cold day, with a hint of winter in the air. When she arrived at Mary's hogan, a wisp of smoke was curling upward from its traditional smoke hole. As she had the morning she'd slept beside the gorge, she parked the Cherokee and got out to wait.

Mary appeared at once, again almost as if she'd been expecting her. "Come in...I have coffee and corncakes prepared for us," she invited.

As they sat cross-legged on piled-up rugs and blankets beside the welcome warmth of Mary's cooking fire, sipping at her strong, black coffee and munching the crisp griddle cakes she'd fried in her blackened iron skillet and doused with syrup, neither of them said very much. At last Kyra broached the subject she'd come to talk about. She quickly found herself pouring out everything.

"I'm going to have David's baby," she told the elderly Navajo woman with tears running down her cheeks, after being assured her words would be held in confidence. "Yet I can't recall our only lovemaking very clearly. All I seem to have retained is this extraordinary dream...."

"What you remember wasn't a dream."

Enunciated in Mary's low-pitched, somewhat husky voice, the assertion had the ring of truth. Yet how could Kyra put any credence in it? David's great-grandfather had conducted the ceremony she remembered. And he'd been dead for several years.

"I...don't understand," she faltered.

The old woman's dark, seemingly fathomless eyes remained firmly fixed on her face. "You and David journeyed to the past," she explained. "You were married there, in the gorge, by my father. I know because I was there, too. I handed you the wedding basket."

In a flash Kyra remembered Mary doing exactly what she claimed, her aged face appearing somewhat younger and astonishingly radiant. Yet she was more confused than ever. "How can that be?" she demanded, almost afraid to speak. "I know about the quantum physics theory that all moments in time exist simultaneously, like the individual pearls on a necklace. Yet it's never actually been demonstrated that we can leap from one to another. Even with the most powerful space hardware available..."

Mary scoffed, though she did it gently. "*You* demonstrated it," she replied with conviction. "What you call 'hardware' isn't necessary. For a handful of us, the way is a tribal secret, handed down to us by our mentors. Yet occasionally others stumble across it, making me wonder if it's an undiscovered talent we all possess. Maybe, for you, your love for David was the determining factor. All I know is that when I entered his presence that day, my father was expecting you."

So matter-of-fact, as if they were talking about the weather, the account left Kyra stunned. Both she and Mary were silent for several more minutes, sipping coffee as Kyra let the rightness of what the older woman had told her sink into her bones like rain in a desert place.

At last she spoke. "I want to believe you," she said softly. "In a way, I *do.* But I still don't understand why David left me in the Cherokee the next morning and came here, to your hogan, to chop wood. Didn't he think I'd remember? Didn't he want me to?"

Mary was a long time answering. "Why don't you ask

him that question?'' she said at last. "He's your husband, though the two of you didn't apply for an official marriage licence.''

The father of my baby, too, Kyra thought. Not to mention the man I love. Yet even as she yearned to follow Mary's advice, she was blocked by the past—specifically by what she believed had been David's mercenary behavior. Her reserve crumbling, she told Mary the story her loved and respected father had told her five years earlier.

The older woman listened impassively, then shook her head. "That doesn't sound like the David I know," she remarked. "Not even when he was young and irresponsible. Maybe you should ask your father if he spoke the truth.''

The possibility that Big Jim had lied in a misguided attempt to keep her focused on law school—perhaps even to prevent her from marrying a half-breed—blew like a fresh breeze through Kyra's consciousness. With it came a burst of energy that freed her from her self-imposed edict that David must confess spontaneously. If he didn't do what her father had accused him of, she realized, how could he possibly know what she was talking about?

Thanking Mary and bidding her goodbye, Kyra drove back to Flagstaff to confront her father. He was in his office at the courthouse, working on the Dale Cargill case. Striding in without pausing to say hello to Jody, she firmly shut the door.

Clearly the look on her face gave him pause. "What is it, gal?" he asked. "Something wrong?"

She gave him a cool, appraising look. "You tell me, Dad," she suggested. "I want to know if the story you handed me five years ago...the one about David taking ten thousand dollars from you to throw me over...contained a grain of truth."

Though he protested that it had, she could see Big Jim's demeanor crumbling. "I have to know," she persisted, refusing to let him off the hook. "Can't you see it means the earth?"

Ultimately, she guessed, the fact that she was still his little girl, the child he'd raised alone following her mother's death, was the deciding factor in convincing him to admit the truth. She obviously loved David. He didn't want her to be unhappy.

"It was for your own good, baby," he admitted, pleading for her understanding. "I wanted you to finish law school. Have the kind of life that would make you happy, instead of shacking up with some half-breed and having yourself a bunch of babies. David was handsome, young and irresponsible. He still had a lot of catting around to do. You'd have fallen through the cracks."

So what if David wasn't ready to settle down? Kyra asked herself. That was then. This is now. Today, he's as solid as a rock. If he hasn't given up on me, maybe we can have a life together.

"It's different now," she replied, the lonely years she'd endured because of her trust in him echoing in her voice. "How could you have done such a thing, knowing how much it would hurt? Though I married Brad on the rebound, it was always David I loved."

Big Jim's face was a mirror to her pain. "You're right...I shouldn't have done it," he agreed. "Though I've come to know that, I've been afraid to say anything. I thought if I told you the truth I'd never see you again."

That might have been true if she hadn't met Henry and Mary Many Horses, she thought. Or spent a night of bliss in David's arms.

Seconds later she was hugging the father who'd injured her, the father she still loved. "That won't happen, Dad," she assured him. "But you need to know something. If it's not too late, I'm going to get David back. He's going to be your son-in-law, the father of your grandchildren. Some of them will look like him, thanks to their Navajo heritage. You'd better make your peace with it."

Bounding down the courthouse stairs from her father's second-floor office, Kyra headed for David's ranch north of town. I won't phone him, she decided. I want to catch him off guard.

To her dismay, when she reached the property, his secretary informed her he'd left that morning in the motor home he used as a home base during lengthy stays out of state, headed for the Lower Brule Reservation in South Dakota. It was the site of his next case.

He was gone.

To make matters worse, Kyra had only a vague idea of where the Lower Brule Reservation was situated. When his secretary tried to get in touch with him via his cellular phone, at her request, the attempt didn't meet with success. "It's possible the battery has gone dead without his knowing it," the woman speculated.

Kyra wasn't content to wait and hope that he'd call her. What she wanted was his arms around her. "Please...tell me what route he planned to take," she begged.

Her expression betraying some knowledge of their difficulties, the woman considered her request and decided in her favor. "When he's headed north, he usually drives up to the Grand Canyon, then travels through Monument Valley before catching Interstate 25," she said. "I know...it's somewhat out of the way. But according to him, he likes to stop and soak up the wonders the Great Spirit placed in this part of the country before leaving it to defend a client elsewhere. He says it gives him a place of peace inside himself from which to operate.''

Something about the woman's tone suggested David was in greater need of inner peace than usual at the moment. If he still cares about me after the way I've treated him, Kyra thought, that's probably my fault.

Getting a detailed description of his motor home along with its tag number, she started in pursuit. He had quite a lead on her, she knew, and kept her eyes peeled for sheriff's deputies as she exceeded the speed limit. She could only hope his secretary was right—that he would pull off somewhere to meditate.

Thanks to the nippy weather, Grand Canyon Village was relatively deserted, in sharp contrast to the crush of visitors it drew during the summer months. There was no sign of David. But then Kyra hadn't expected to find him in a tourist hangout. Given his probable route, she guessed, if he'd stopped anywhere in the park, it would be near its eastern boundary.

Outside, the temperature was dropping, and she switched on the Cherokee's heater. A moment later it started to snow, in light, granular flakes. Turning east at the canyon's rim, she drove more slowly, winding through every overlook's parking area and scanning the license tag of each recreational vehicle she passed.

At the easternmost overlook on the canyon's south rim, which was deserted except for him, David was seated on a rocky ledge with a down-lined vest zipped over his corduroy shirt and gray, cotton-knit turtleneck, gazing into the awe-inspiring chasm the Colorado River had created before the first man and woman had set foot in what would one day be Arizona.

Unwilling to think about the wasteland his life would

become if Kyra returned to Kansas City as planned, he tried to focus on the stunning view before him, the ponderosa pines' pungent evergreen scent. With all his heart, that night on the Namingas' porch swing, he'd wanted to hang on to her physically—tell her about the group of one woman and two men in the sand painting and ask for her reaction.

Instead, he'd decided to defer to his great-grandfather's counsel.

"If you separate after this night, your woman must come to you," the old man had told him when they'd talked prior to the wedding ceremony. "Otherwise, she'll miss the lesson your problems hold for her. The insights of trust and respect for what her heart tells her will be lost."

In deference to the old man's advice, he'd left for Lower Brule without phoning her, though everything in his heart had militated against it. As he stared at the glorious frieze of rose-rock cathedrals that comprised the canyon's north rim and the light snow that had begun to fall, he didn't pay any attention to the utility vehicle that pulled up and parked beside his motor home. Nor was he aware of Kyra's light footsteps as she approached, thanks to the chill wind that was whistling through the gorge below.

Startled when one of her boots crunched a piece of gravel directly behind him, he got to his feet and found himself staring in disbelief. Incredibly, Kyra had followed him. She was looking at him with love written all over her face.

With a muffled groan, he enfolded her. As they clung together in the frosty air, lovers who'd come too close to losing each other a second time, their kisses were passionate, a little desperate.

When finally she could speak, though she was still crushed tightly in his arms, Kyra confided that she'd remembered their wedding in the gorge. "Your grandmother helped me understand what had taken place," she admitted. "But it was there in my head all along. I want to honor our vows, David."

"So do I." Deep and a little rough, his voice was on the verge of breaking. "You can't imagine how difficult it's been, wanting to remind you of our wedding and not doing it. My great-grandfather advised me to let you make the first move."

To think she almost hadn't made it. Thanks to Mary Many Horses and her father's confession, they would spend their lives together. "You may as well know that I plan to insist on a license and a civil ceremony," she told him, dimpling in the way she had so often when they'd been almost lovers, during their first infatuation. "That way, when our baby comes..."

Amazed and overjoyed to learn that he'd be a father, David covered her mouth with kisses. Seconds later he was sweeping her up into his arms and carrying her into the motor home.

"I want to make love to you," he confessed, depositing her on the down comforter that covered his bed and pulling off her boots. "So much that I'm on fire with it. With our child growing inside you, do you think it would be all right?"

"Of course." Holding out her arms, Kyra welcomed him into her embrace. "We won't have to abstain until some-time in the last trimester, darling," she informed him, un-zipping his down vest and unbuttoning his shirt so he could peel them off along with his turtleneck, revealing the bronze skin and dark chest hair she loved. "Since I plan to quit my job in Kansas City and become your law partner, I have a million and one the years we've wasted."

* * *

That afternoon, in the cozy confines of his motor home, Kyra and David made love with a richness and tender majesty she'd never dreamed the act could possess. Not even their incredibly tantalizing, soulful communion in the gorge on their wedding night could compare to it. Maybe that was because, by now, they'd become inextricably intertwined, parents of the same beloved unborn baby.

When she suggested the idea to David after their ascent had subsided, he agreed with all the love a woman could want shining in his face. Meanwhile, outside the motor home's windows, the snow had begun to fall more thickly, in large, delicate flakes.

"I know it would be something of a bother, getting dressed again, but I'd love to go out in it," Kyra suggested. "I've been away from Arizona so much the past few years. Now that it's going to be home again, I want to see the canyon in its winter dress."

There'd be time to cuddle beneath his down comforter again later—a whole lifetime filled with such moments. "Whatever would please you, White Shell Woman," David whispered, gently kissing her mouth.

It was only when they stood wrapped in their winter jackets and each other's arms, gazing past the canyon's rim at the way its glorious snow-topped rock formations seemed to blend into the overhanging clouds, that a little frown drew David's dark brows together.

"Can you tell me now what you wouldn't, before... about the thing that's been keeping us apart?" he asked.

When she complied, explaining everything, he was furious. "Lucky for him Jim Frakes is your father," he said grimly. "Or I'd punch his lights out."

Instead of defending her dad, Kyra replied that she was angry at him, too. "I blame him...*and* myself for believing him," she confessed.

In response, David assumed some responsibility as well. "I shouldn't have bought into his contention that if I disappeared from your life, I'd be doing you a favor," he said. "According to him, with me in tow, you wouldn't have finished law school."

Kyra was silent a moment. "Why didn't you at least say goodbye?" she asked, a sheen of tears suddenly glittering beneath her lashes. "When you disappeared like that, it was like the bottom fell out of my world."

"Ah, babe...I'm so sorry I hurt you." Pulling her more tightly against him, David did his best to comfort her. "I wish to God, the Great Spirit or whoever rules the universe, that I'd explained everything to you instead of believing your father when he said a clean break would be best," he said. "I wanted to...more than you'll ever guess. Unfortunately I wanted to start my own law practice, too. I *needed* to, in order to pay off my debts and support a family someday. I knew it would be a rough go for a while. I didn't want to derail your education or saddle you with supporting me for the duration. Then I heard you got married. I thought it was all over with us."

Though he wasn't ready to forgive Big Jim, Kyra made it plain that she didn't plan to cut herself off from her erring parent. "Somehow, given time, we'll resolve this," she predicted, nestling against the warmth of David's body. "What matters most is that you and I and our precious baby will be together."

Epilogue

On Christmas day, fourteen months later, five-month-old James David Yazzie lay on the exquisite Navajo rug in front of his parents' huge, stone fireplace, waving his arms and legs as he stared at the lighted tree, which twinkled like a vision of fairyland. Thanks to his most recent meal at his mother's breast, a full tummy contributed to his contentment.

Watching him with pleasure from one of the chocolate brown, piqué velvet sofas as, holding hands, they listened to a Mozart glass-harmonica compact disc in lieu of traditional carols, his mother and father were awaiting an important guest for the holiday meal. Already the delicious scent of roasting turkey stuffed with Navajo-style corn bread dressing pervaded the house, adding to the aura of well-being there.

Only one question waited in the wings, demanding to be resolved. Since his civil marriage to Big Jim Frakes's daughter in South Dakota, David hadn't seen the retired prosecutor, though Kyra had kept in touch with him. Now he was coming over, paying them a Christmas visit at Kyra's request.

Though he felt somewhat uncomfortable about the situation, David had agreed to entertain his son's repentant grandfather at their dinner table in honor of Jamie's first holiday.

Dale Cargill had been convicted of Ben Monongye's murder and was serving time in state prison. Meanwhile, Leonard Naminga's five-year-old conviction for DUI, manslaughter and grand theft auto had been reversed with Big Jim's help, in addition to the good offices of Tom Hanrahan, the new Coconino County Attorney.

Under questioning, in the hope of mitigating his sentence, Dale had admitted hitting the elderly couple Leonard had been accused of killing as he'd started home from a bar where he'd drunk excessively. Staggering back to the establishment in question, he'd called the police to say his pickup had been stolen. Subsequently, he'd phoned his foreman for a ride home.

As it turned out, Leonard had arrived at the scene of the crash on foot, even more tanked-up than Dale, and mistakenly thought the elderly couple needed a push. A decent enough sort despite his alcoholism, he'd gotten behind the wheel of Dale's vehicle and attempted to help.

When the police had arrived at the scene and arrested him, Dale hadn't come forward to save him. Released from prison and the brutal indignities he'd suffered there, Leonard was living with Paul, Julie and their two children. According to Julie, he'd given up alcohol. Recently he'd begun to speak again, enunciating a few simple phrases and questions.

Big Jim's arrival was an awkward moment for everyone but little Jamie, who was oblivious to the tensions involved. He didn't catch his mother's sigh of relief as his father held out a hand in welcome and his grandfather took it, giving it a firm shake.

Given that Kyra and David had been out of town since shortly after their son's birth, thanks to an important case David had taken in Washington State, it was the first time Jim Frakes had seen his namesake except for several visits he'd paid to Kyra in the hospital.

Tears filled the older man's eyes as Kyra scooped up her little boy and held him up for inspection. After rhapsodizing over what a beautiful child Jamie was, he asked if they could sit down a moment and talk before breaking out the holiday cheer.

"The fact is, I have a proposal to make," he said.

Her heart overflowing, Kyra watched her husband's hard gaze soften as her father, whom he'd once liked and admired, suggested he make up for the ten-thousand-dollar lie he'd told by contributing a similar amount of cash to David's favorite charity, a foundation he'd set up to provide legal help to indigent Native Americans.

"You might call it a kind of 'bride price' in reverse," Big Jim explained nervously, as if he half expected that the amends he was proposing would be rejected.

Instead of tossing the proposal back in his face or attempting to rehash the past, David smiled slightly at his father-in-law's allusion to the Navajo custom whereby a suitor provides the father of his intended with an appropriate number of horses in exchange for the honor of marrying his daughter.

"In our case the father deserves to pay, not the husband," Kyra's father added. "I hope you'll forgive me, David...and that we can begin again as friends and equals. I can't think of a worthier man to be my daughter's spouse and helpmate."

A moment later, the "bride price" Big Jim had offered

had been accepted. Everyone was hugging everyone else, including Jamie, who'd somehow managed to get in the middle of it. His gurgle of delight at being surrounded by so much love had everyone agreeing that he was priceless.

* * * * *

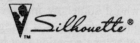

Take 4 bestselling love stories FREE

Plus get a FREE surprise gift!

Special Limited-time Offer

Mail to Silhouette Reader Service™

> 3010 Walden Avenue
> P.O. Box 1867
> Buffalo, N.Y. 14240-1867

YES! Please send me 4 free Silhouette Romance™ novels and my free surprise gift. Then send me 6 brand-new novels every month, which I will receive months before they appear in bookstores. Bill me at the low price of $2.67 each plus 25¢ delivery and applicable sales tax, if any.* That's the complete price and a savings of over 10% off the cover prices—quite a bargain! I understand that accepting the books and gift places me under no obligation ever to buy any books. I can always return a shipment and cancel at any time. Even if I never buy another book from Silhouette, the 4 free books and the surprise gift are mine to keep forever.

215 BPA A3UT

Name	(PLEASE PRINT)	
Address	Apt. No.	
City	State	Zip

This offer is limited to one order per household and not valid to present Silhouette Romance™ subscribers. *Terms and prices are subject to change without notice. Sales tax applicable in N.Y.

USROM-696   ©1990 Harlequin Enterprises Limited

SILHOUETTE WOMEN KNOW ROMANCE WHEN THEY SEE IT.

And they'll see it on **ROMANCE CLASSICS**, the new 24-hour TV channel devoted to romantic movies and original programs like the special **Romantically Speaking-Harlequin® Goes Prime Time.**

Romantically Speaking-Harlequin® Goes Prime Time introduces you to many of your favorite romance authors in a program developed exclusively for Harlequin® and Silhouette® readers.

Watch for **Romantically Speaking-Harlequin® Goes Prime Time** beginning in the summer of 1997.

*If you're not receiving **ROMANCE CLASSICS**, call your local cable operator or satellite provider and ask for it today!*

ROMANCE CLASSICS

Escape to the network of your dreams.

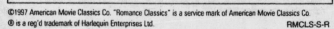

You've been waiting for him all your life....
Now your Prince has finally arrived!

In fact, *three* handsome princes
are coming your way in

ROYAL WEDDINGS

A delightful new miniseries by **LISA KAYE LAUREL**
about three bachelor princes who find happily-ever-
after with three small-town women!

Coming in September 1997—THE PRINCE'S BRIDE

Crown Prince Erik Anders would do anything for his
country—even plan a pretend marriage to his lovely
castle caretaker. But could he convince the king, and
the rest of the world, that his proposal was real—before
his cool heart melted for his small-town "bride"?

Coming in November 1997—THE PRINCE'S BABY

Irresistible Prince Whit Anders was shocked to
discover that the summer romance he'd had years
ago had resulted in a very royal baby! Now that
pretty Drew Davis's secret was out, could her kiss
turn the sexy prince into a full-time dad?

**Look for prince number three in the exciting
conclusion to ROYAL WEDDINGS,
coming in 1998—only from**

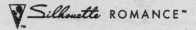

Silhouette ROMANCE™

Daniel MacGregor is at it again…

New York Times bestselling author

NORA ROBERTS

introduces us to a new generation of MacGregors
as the lovable patriarch of the illustrious MacGregor
clan plays matchmaker again, this time to his three
gorgeous granddaughters in

THE
MacGREGOR
BRIDES

From Silhouette Books

Don't miss this brand-new continuation of Nora Roberts's
enormously popular *MacGregor* miniseries.

Available November 1997 at your favorite retail outlet.

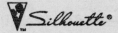